No Place Like Home

Keith Hellwig

No part of this publication may be reproduced, stored in a retrieval system, or transmitted, in any form or by any means, electronic, mechanical, photocopying, recording, or otherwise, without the written permission of the author.

First published by Dog Ear Publishing
4010 W. 86th Street, Ste H
Indianapolis, IN 46268
www.dogearpublishing.net

ISBN: 978-145752-871-2

This book is printed on acid-free paper.

Printed in the United States of America

4:30pm

"There's no place like home, there's no place like home, there's no place like home." The mantra repeated itself in the Captain's head. "The Wizard of Oz" was an autumn ritual for his family; they had watched it last night for perhaps the fifteenth time.

Now the Captain sat with two other officers, handcuffed, in the Social Worker's office of Housing Unit Sixteen. The side of his head throbbed where he had been hit with a mop handle. His eye socket was swollen shut, and he was sure his nose was broken, but at least it wasn't bleeding anymore. He probed his teeth with his tongue and came away with the taste of blood, but he could feel no gaps. His ribs ached from being kicked, and for a moment, he was glad for the spare weight around his middle. He forced his attention away from the pain of his injuries, the moans of his fellow officers, and the rancid smell of sweat and fear; he closed his good eye and focused on those last hours with his family — and Dorothy and her witches, good and bad:

His wife, Maura, an artist, was making a preliminary sketch for a new painting, looking up only occasionally to watch Dorothy and her friends. His daughters, LeAnn and Marie, were intermittently pestering each other, playing with Maggie, the blue merle Collie, watching the movie, and chatting. Most of what they said to each other was lost in a jumble of rushed, slurred words, but occasionally he caught a bit about teachers, friends, and — increasingly — boys.

The Captain smiled at the thought, and the stretching of his lips brought a sharp pain that popped his good eye open. Two inmates circled the room like sharks preparing for a kill. The one with "Q-ball" tattooed on his neck leaned against the closed door, his arms crossed. The one with the burn-scarred face checked the handcuffs on the youngest officer, Kyle Hennricks, who made the mistake of looking at him and received a back-hand across the face. "Don' be lookin' at me, Mother-fucker," he growled. The Captain fixed his gaze on Hennricks, shook his head every-so-slightly, and slowly closed his good eye, as though to say: no point in looking for an angle right now — take your thoughts elsewhere.

The Captain had been grateful, as he watched the "Wizard," that the end of autumn was near. Soon he'd rake the leaves from the Maple trees that covered his yard. He'd put the chore off too long the year before, and snow had covered the ground and the leaves, creating a huge mess in spring. Maura had reminded him of it all winter; he didn't want to put up with that again. On his coming days off, he vowed, he'd clean up nature's mess. If only there were to be days off coming. The Captain opened his good eye. The scar-faced inmate was fooling with Hennricks' cuffs, pulling at them roughly as though to test them, but obviously, more than anything, testing Hennricks.

Hennricks sat with his eyes closed, his head down, arms limp, just as he should — for the moment. The Captain closed his eye and traveled "home" again. Behind his eighty-year-old house, a small river ran. Across the river, several hiking trails traversed the woods. He and Maura had been attracted by the large lot and the privacy it offered, in the middle of a city. They had bought the house when LeAnn was a baby; Marie had come along four years later. A tree swing, a wooden play set, a sand box — and another swing-set — had for years made the girls' place a second home for many friends. It was a good home.

Somebody coughed, and the Captain's good eye popped open. It was Phil Adams, the other officer. For no apparent reason, the scar-faced inmate had landed a kick on Adams's kidney.

Adams sat passively, his head down, eyes barely open behind a cracked pair of horn-rimmed glasses. The inmate drew his foot back for another kick, yanking unintended words from the Captain's bloodied mouth. "There's no need for that!"

The inmate whirled to face the Captain. "Q, check that other Mo'fucker while I deal with the Captain."

As the scar-faced inmate strode toward him, the Captain saw the flash of a shank in his hand. It was an ugly weapon, fashioned out of a piece of bed rail, it's edges scraped sharp and brought to a point — no doubt by rubbing on the concrete cell floor or wall. The Captain thought of Maura, LeAnn and Marie. Like Dorothy, the Captain wanted to go home.

*   *   *

CHAPTER I

AS THE CREDITS HAD ROLLED on Dorothy and her friends, the Captain had put on his uniform, gun, and vest for his part-time job as a cop and said goodnight to his family. "I'll see you all tomorrow afternoon when I get done at the prison. I have the next few days off, and we'll do something as a family." LeAnn rolled her eyes. Maura squeezed LeAnn's hand. By some magic, his wife was still able to talk his eldest into family outings.

The Captain put in only a few hours a week as a road officer in the small village of Campbell, about fifteen miles west of his home. The second job allowed Maura to work on her art and be a stay-at-home Mom, and he enjoyed the work, though the short nights of sleep made getting up in the morning to go to the joint a bit of a challenge.

Maura was worth it. She was the most beautiful woman the Captain had ever known, with long dark hair and the exotic look of a Gypsy; her dad's parents were first-generation Americans from Romania. After twenty-five years of marriage and two kids, she was as slim and trims as the day they'd met — and every bit as smart, comforting, and inspiring. As an artist, Maura had recently started making a name for herself.

That night, as usual, the house was dark and quiet when he returned from Campbell at midnight. In her sleep, Maura turned to snuggle him. And then the alarm rang.

1

At 4:45, the Captain rose to shower, shave and dress. He put on his Corrections uniform, always cleaned and pressed, and as he buckled the black basket-weave leather duty belt, he automatically checked his equipment, running his hands around the belt. He knew by feel where everything belonged: handcuffs, maglight, glove pouch, key rings, radio case and badge were all in place. Over the left pocket flap of his white uniform shirt, his gold name-tag might as well have been blank. Nobody ever called him anything but Captain, or sometimes simply "Cap" Two ink pens jutted from the pocket, their chrome barrels glinting. In the bathroom mirror, he adjusted his shirt collar so that the shiny-gold double bars stood at the right angle. Captains wore two; lieutenants, the second-in-command among line officers, wore one, also on white shirts. The officers who ranked under them wore blue shirts with their rank on their sleeves: a Department of Corrections patch on the left shoulder and an American flag on the right.

The Captain put on the dreaded bifocals. He couldn't help seeing them as a sign of weakness and age, though Maura called them distinguished. He was thankful, in any case, that he could see well enough without them. Unlike most people his age, it was mostly his long-distance vision that was going. He could still read in decent light without glasses.

He cocked his head and got a satisfying "pop" from his neck. He looked pretty good: six-foot four inches tall, and weighing-in at two hundred and seventy-five. He had Hazel eyes, and his "dishwater-blond hair" was graying and thinning a bit. He attributed the hair loss to one of two things: either he was simply getting old, or, number two; he had scraped away his hair from smacking his head getting in and out of cars dozens of times a day. In his youth, his hair had hung to his shoulders. He often joked that it was the only thing about him that was thinning. But he'd never been skinny. The extra weight he carried had always been there, and he had learned to accept it, as he was learning to accept the inevitable changes of time.

He clipped the ridiculous black necktie to his collar, a reminder of the arbitrary power of Security Director William Thorson. No sooner had Thorson promoted and transferred in to NWSP — the North Wood State Prison — than he'd dictated the new rule that all captains and lieutenants would wear neck ties with their winter uniforms. North Wood was the only prison in the state with such a dress code. The gold tie clip that his wife had given him for their thirtieth anniversary helped mitigate his irritation with the tie, but as he gazed at his reflection, his fingers fumbling to attach clip to tie, he thought, "another bunch of bullshit from a petty dictator."

He put the lid down on the toilet, propped up one foot, and leaned down to pull on his boots. He had found a pair of black hiking boots that fit like slippers — the most comfortable thing he wore. He dressed in the bathroom to avoid waking Maura, and it was his boots that used to make the most noise. He inevitably dropped one if he sat on the bed to pull them on, and if he tried to put them on standing up, he hopped around like a deranged gorilla. This way, using the toilet as footstool, allowed for a calm precision, right down through tying the laces.

He made his way by habit through the darkened house, grabbing from the entry-hall closet on his way out a dark-blue, waist-length uniform coat. Like his shirt, the coat was adorned on each epaulet with Captain's bars. He pulled the fur collar tight around his throat and went out into the cold, crisp autumn morning.

On his way out of town, he stopped at a convenience store and topped off his tank for the thirty-minute trip to the prison. Then he pulled up to the front-door of the store, leaving the car running while he went inside, so the heater could kick in. He grabbed a cup of coffee for himself and three bagels: one for him, one for his lieutenant, and one for the third-shift captain. It was a mission of mercy. Lieutenant Scott Gaines wouldn't have the money to get himself anything other than a cup of coffee on the way to work. He paid too much in alimony to his two ex-wives and the four kids he'd fathered. Come to think of it, Lt. Gaines probably wouldn't even have time to stop for coffee today. He'd had his three older kids for the night and had to drop them back off at his first ex-wife's house. Once he'd started buying for Lt. Gaines, the Captain had also started buying for Captain Schmidt, the third shift Captain who wouldn't say no to a snack before heading home. So, pretty much every day, the Captain was springing for three breakfasts.

After clearing the neat, cookie-cutter neighborhoods on the west side of the city, his drive to the prison ran twenty miles along twisting country roads. A state forest spread on both sides for most of the way, and on more than one occasion, he had slammed on his breaks, narrowly missing a whitetail deer leaping out of the woods. So he watched ahead for suicidal bucks, while he listened to the news on the radio.

At least the election was over, and he didn't have to listen to Alan Colmes whine about the "religious right" and the doom they would wreak. But he tired just as quickly of a report of Muslim fanatics taking hostages. The older he got, the less stomach he had for strife from home and abroad. He pushed in a CD, noting the irony of fleeing serious news for the reckless rhythms of his youth. George Thorogood blared "Bad to the Bone," and he sang along:

> "On the day I was born,
> The Nurses all gathered around.
> And gazed in wide wonder,
> At the joy they had found.
> The head nurse spoke up,
> And said "leave this one alone!"
> She could tell right away,
> I was bad to the bone!"

He chuckled out loud. How odd it was that he was wearing a uniform, working full time in a prison and part-time as a cop. He had been one of the kids in his high school class whom everyone thought of as "bad to the bone." In a class of ninety students, he'd stood out not only because of his size, but also because of the attention he drew from the police chief. A partier, he'd been accused of lots of things, of which he was mostly innocent. Chief Vandenburg made it a point to call him out of class at least once a week to question him. It was almost always, "Someone saw a car like yours . . . ," followed by questions about some minor crime for which there was no suspect. He'd be sent back to class after a few minutes, his reputation damaged: the teachers figured him a hood; the hoods figured him a snitch. He was neither. But in a community of twelve hundred, most people took their cues from the authorities and thought they knew everything.

Now, years later, and a hundred miles away, few people knew of, or would have believed, his reputation as a troublemaker. He had put it behind him.

Among the nearly naked trees, the harsh glow of the prison's lights met him two miles out. Though NWSP was twenty miles from the nearest city, it lit the sky as bright with artificial daylight as Milwaukee or Green Bay. Five sets of hi-mast Halogen lights poked skyward from the prison grounds, bathing them — and the globe of moisture around them — in a blue-tinted aura.

Built in 1962, the prison had originally been a boy's reformatory, the North Woods Juvenile Detention Facility. The Captain had been there three times by the time he was seventeen, but not because of those run-ins with Chief Vandenburg. His High School Band played an annual Christmas concert at juvie, and as a trombone player, he'd looked at the kids in the audience and been thankful that he got to leave! Maybe that's why he'd never done anything that landed him more than a night in jail. That and a wrestling coach who taught him to talk about what was eating him.

The boy's reformatory was converted to a men's prison twelve years after it was built, with the addition of two twenty-foot fences, seven gun towers at uneven intervals, the hi-mast lights, and an armed perimeter patrol. He took a job there soon after. He never could shake the feeling that the manned gun towers were out of place in the tranquil setting, but then again, where wouldn't seven gun towers seem out of place? The double fence, likewise, communicated ferocity out of step with the gentle forest. Topped with razor wire, the fences were designed to tear an escaping man's flesh from his body. The last escape had been seventeen years before; since the three last gun towers and the second twenty-foot fence had been added, nobody had escaped. That didn't stop cons from making plans, though. The Captain drove his SUV through the intersection with the perimeter road and into the staff parking lot, where he cut the engine.

Gazing at the towers in the hot blue light of the prison's pre-dawn, he indulged for a moment his memories of the last serious escape plan that could have gone very bad. It had happened about two months ago, and already the memory was fading from staff's memory, becoming a thing of the past, much the same as Pearl Harbor or 9-11. The consequences, for at least a few families, could have been as devastating.

The Captain had been writing officer evaluations, and had just opened a fresh can of diet Coke when Sergeant John Murphy called. "Captain, I got an inmate here that has been telling me a story you might want to hear."

"OK, Murph, what do you think you have?" the Captain said, with an inaudible sigh. Most "plans" that inmates snitched about were ninety-nine percent crap. He pushed the evals'   off to the side of his desk and took a sip of the soda.

"It's inmate Fred Barnes. He wants to talk to you real quick. He says it's about an escape — and plans to hurt an officer. He's always been good for the stuff he's told me."

The Captain sat back, took his glasses off, pinched the bridge of his nose, and closed his eyes. If Sgt. Murphy said Barnes had good information, then you could bet your life that he did. Murph had served six years in the Marines, enlisting at seventeen and doing two tours of duty in Vietnam by the time he was twenty-three. When the Marines wouldn't let him return to Vietnam, he'd switched to the Army, which sent him to Intelligence School and gave him two more tours in 'Nam. He eventually became an Army Ranger and concluded his military career after serving in the first Gulf War. The Captain, twelve year's Murph's junior, had been his field training officer when he came to the prison, and the older rookie's professionalism and military bearing had impressed him from the start. Now fifty-nine years old, with thick, graying hair and a pot belly, Murph still kept his shoes spit-shined and his uniform creases sharp enough to cut soft butter.

The Captain stretched his legs out in front of him to full length, and his knees cracked at the joints. It felt good to work the kinks out. "Send him up to admin' with the story that he has to see his social worker. That way, if any other inmates hear he's coming up, he has an excuse. I'll get him before he gets to the admin' building."

It would take Barnes about ten minutes to walk from the unit to the security office, where he'd be searched before being brought in. The Captain called the control center to let them know what was up, then checked Barnes's file. He was a thirty-one-year-old short-timer, with less than two years left to serve for stealing a car. He had served time before, a total of more than ten years, but he didn't have much of a disciplinary record and had flown under the radar for the three years he'd been locked up this time. The Captain was returning Barnes's file to the cabinet when Officer Cunningham escorted the inmate into the office.

The Captain turned to meet him. Sizing-him-up, the Captain saw that Barnes looked the part of an outlaw biker who had spent a lot of his life behind bars. His heavily muscled arms testified to his physical strength, and from the Swastika tattooed on his forehead to the "White Power" covering his right arm, it was apparent where his sympathies lay.

"Good Morning, Mr. Barnes," the Captain said, nodding politely. "Sgt. Murphy told me you wanted to talk to me? C'mon in and have a seat." He walked to his desk and sat.   He motioned Barnes to have a seat across the desk from his.

"Now, I aint no snitch," Barnes started, still standing, "but I don't wanna see anyone get hurt. There's some serious shit bein' hatched." He looked around the office — at the backs of the photographs on the Captain's desk, and beyond the desk, at the statute and rule books on a cold, gray metal bookshelf, courtesy of the inmate industries shop. There were no frills in the large office. The Lieutenant's desk was a mirror image of the Captain's, each with a computer, monitor, desk calendar, and telephone. The family pictures and other personal touches left the desks at shift change — shoved into plastic bags to be replaced by those of the incoming captain and lieutenant.

Any time an inmate started out, "Now, I aint no snitch . . . ," he was revealing that he was, in fact, a snitch, well aware he was breaking the "inmate code." The Captain shook his head, though, to reaffirm Barnes's contention. Once again, he told Barnes to have a seat and the inmate sat, with a final glance at the door behind him. "OK, so what's this all about?" the Captain asked.

Barnes faced the Captain, leaning forward with his elbows on his knees, the "O-W-E-R" of "power" stark against his pale forearm: "You remember Franklin that left about a month ago? He and Klien have a plan to help Klien get out."

The Captain thought back, trying to conjure a memory of Franklin. It didn't take long for the memories of parolees to melt together. But he could picture Franklin, a short, curly-haired brute who had been a pain in the ass, provoking minor hassles with black inmates, never enough to get him hurt, but plenty to keep everyone around him tense. Franklin and Klien, like Barnes, were bikers. Franklin had gotten a mandatory release five weeks ago, and they were glad to be rid of him. Klien, in Unit Nine, still had a few years to go.

The plan, according to Barnes, was that Klien was going to hurt himself intentionally — "bust a finger or somethin'" — to get an officer to take him to St. Bernadette Hospital, where Franklin would be waiting with his girlfriend, three guns and two stolen cars. Franklin would shoot the officer in the back of the head, make sure he was dead, and then he and the girl would head off, each in their own car. Klein would follow in the other car, through the downtown area to the highway, about a mile away. The shooting would draw police attention from downtown, giving them time to rob two drugstores on their way. They'd score some Oxy, some methodone, perhaps a few vicodin, and whatever money was on hand in the registers. The drugs would be easy to move and would bring top dollar. Once they hit the highway, they'd go in opposite directions, meeting up later to divide the drugs and money. It was supposed to go down in less than two days.

The Captain made notes on his computer, listening intently. He remained silent when Barnes was done, cocking his head at the tough little inmate. "How do I know you're telling the truth?" he finally asked.

"Cap, I aint gonna let no one die. I couldn't stand myself if I did. I been jailin' for ten years, and I got me a wife and kid. I just wanna do the right thing. These officers been treating me good, and I know they have a job to do. That job don't include dying. "

The Captain stood up and held his hand out to shake. "Mr. Barnes, thank you for letting me in on this. You were right: this is some serious shit being hatched."

As Barnes returned to his unit, the Captain walked down the hall to Security Chief Thorson's office. William Thorson was the type of man who would have donned jack-boots and a black uniform with lightning bolts on it during World War II. He would have clicked his heels with a "Sieg Heil."   "What is it?" he said brusquely, turning from his big window as the Captain entered.

Thorson was five feet four inches tall, though his carefully coifed hair added another inch or two. He wore a bushy "Mario Brothers" mustache and a suit that probably came off the "Junior's" rack at J.C. Penny.   Everyone knew that there was no love lost between the Captain and the Security Director, but Thorson was boss, and the Captain knew enough to tread carefully in his presence. He kept his distance — it made Thorson nervous to have the big man towering over him — and slid into a straight-back chair when Thorson nodded a surly permission. Thorson had started a couple of years behind the Captain, and had elevated his career by stepping on the backs of others. The Captain knew he was a vindictive little prick, and Thorson knew the Captain knew.

"I think we have something developing, sir," the Captain said.

The Security Director listened with his chin cupped in his hand, as though a modern-day Socrates.

The Captain was careful to clue Thorson in to what needed to be done without seeming to be suggesting anything and he came away with a feeling of relief at having received the orders he needed while causing no offense. All in all, a good day with Thorson.

Back in his office, the Captain called the Unit Nine sergeant and told him that he was coming down to pick up Klien, then radioed two officers to meet him there. He went out to the parking lot behind the admin' building and climbed into a state car for the half-mile drive. Inside the fence, the prison looked like a sprawling college campus: sixteen inmate housing units spread over a thousand acres cleared from the state forest. He cruised past the school and maintenance complex, the inmate Metal Stamping industry, and the barracks that served as the receiving unit for new inmates. He parked behind Unit Nine.

The two officers and the Unit sergeant had already cleared the inmate dayroom. All he told them was that he was going to place Klien in segregation pending an investigation; the officers and sergeant looked at him expectantly, but that was all they were going to get. ""Room twenty six," the sergeant said.

The officers walked behind the Captain to Klein's room and waited quietly as he looked in the door window. Klien was alone, sitting on his bed and leaning against the wall with his eyes closed, apparently dozing. The Captain used his master key and opened the door. "Klien, I need you to come out of your room and place your hands on the wall." Klien lunged up off his bed, ready to fight.

Behind the Captain, the two officers filled the doorway. "C'mon out and keep your hands where we can see them," the Captain said. The two officers moved to positions next to him.

"What's this all about?" Klein said. He was wiry and lean, taller than Barnes, and his colorfully tattooed wrists stuck out of his prison greens, his big fists balled. "Some motherfucker drop a dime on me?"

"Do what the officers tell you and nothing else," the Captain said. "Any move you make without being told will be considered an act of aggression and dealt with accordingly. You're being placed in segregation. I'll explain everything when I get you to Unit Fourteen. Do you understand?" Klien stared hard at the Captain for a couple of seconds. The officers had their hands up in a defensive position, ready to spring.   "Just go with the program," the Captain said. "Don't get yourself jammed-up by making us do something."

"This is some bullshit," Klein said, as he turned to face the wall. One of the officers cuffed his hands behind his back and took him out of the cell, where they pat searched him.

Then they led him outside, an officer on each arm and the Captain directly behind him, and loaded him into a white van. At a strip-cell in segregation, they took off the handcuffs and searched him naked. While he was donning a bright orange Seg' jumpsuit, the Captain asked, "Do you know why you're here?"

"I got an idea," Klien scowled. "Someone dropped a dime over the hooch on the rec' yard."

"What's your side of the story?" the Captain asked casually.

"Shit wasn't mine. I stole some yeast from the kitchen to help make it, but the shit wasn't mine."

"Whose was it then?"

"Man, I aint no snitch, but you might wanna talk with Barnes. He's always into some kind of shit."

"I'll check into it." The Captain was relieved that Klien had no clue about the escape investigation, but it was obvious that he and Barnes had a grudge, which might cast doubt on Barnes's claim. Something more to check out.

Thorson, meanwhile, had made a call to Franklin's parole agent and learned that he had never reported to her; she'd had a judge sign a fugitive warrant for his arrest. As a parole violator, his property could be searched without a warrant.

In Klien's cell, officers found the address of Franklin's girl-friend, Mimi Curtain, and police arrested both Franklin and Curtain at her house the next morning. In the bedroom, they found a pink diary entitled "Escape Diary." Curtain, a thirty-year-old single mother of four, had started the diary while Franklin was in prison. In loopy, back-slanting handwriting, she'd detailed the plan, just as Barnes had told the Captain, starting with Klien busting a finger. They'd even specified that it would probably be Officer Dave Wilkins who would take Klien to St. Bernadette — and die there. Curtain was supposed to wait between the stolen cars in the emergency lot, and when Officer Wilkins got out and bent to open the back door, she'd call out and distract him so Franklin could shoot him in the back of the head. While Franklin unlocked Klein's cuffs, Curtain would make a frantic 911 call. They figured all five officers on patrol in the city would respond. A half mile from the interstate, on the way out of town, Klein and Franklin would simultaneously rob two drug stores that sat across the road from each other. They'd shoot at least one person in each store to add to the pandemonium, and escape to the interstate, heading in opposite directions. The meet-up to split drugs and profits would come a week later, and they'd plan the next heist.

At 9:30 a.m. on the appointed day, Klein, still in segregation and none the wiser that the jig was up, wedged his little finger into a ventilation grate and snapped it at the knuckle. Screaming in pain, he demanded to go to the hospital. To his surprise, a nurse from the infirmary simply came to segregation and, under the watch of two officers, taped his finger and gave him some Tylenol. At the top of his lungs and to no avail, he threatened everyone from the warden to the nurse with a lawsuit.

The second-shift Captain finally went to Klien's cell and told him, "Franklin said to say hi and tell you he won't be making it to visit you." Klein sat on his Seg' bed, cradling his throbbing finger, tears running down his cheeks. He was taken to the local hospital the next day, under heavy armed guard, then transported to a maximum security prison where he would most likely remain for the next fifteen years.

Following the escape attempt, staff had become super vigilant. They'd realized how vulnerable they were.

Today, though, it worried the Captain that his staff was slipping into a "stand-by" mode once again. There was an old adage: "We run the prison because the inmates let us." At any given time, less than one hundred staff controlled up to seventeen hundred inmates. All it took was a minor spark to ignite a major flame, and while many of the rules seemed petty, they were in place to put out the embers.

A horn honked, startling the Captain. A white prison van circled the paved perimeter road that skirted the parking lot, its exhaust visible in the cold morning air. It took the Captain a second to return the sergeant's wave from the van and to realize he was sitting in his cooling car and he'd better get his ass in gear and get to work. As he stepped out into the damp pre-dawn cold to walk the fifty yards to the gatehouse, he struggled to pull on the attitude appropriate for work.

He'd worked for the Department of Corrections for more than twenty-five years, rising from a blue-shirted Correctional Officer to a white-shirted Correctional Captain, seeing the swing in corrections from a rehabilitation system in which each inmate had a job or school assignment to an overcrowded human ware-house in which many inmates had no assignments or responsi-bilities and wanted nothing more than to sit in the day-rooms watching soap operas and cartoons. While the rest of the world fretted about heat bills, car payments, mortgages and kids, the inmates worried about whether Wily Coyote would catch that pesky roadrunner or — more important to most — whether Sonya would sleep with her cousin on "As the World Grinds." It was important to the Captain that his work should mean some-thing, and the way corrections was going, he had to psych himself up each morning to recapture the faith.

The Captain went through a gate in the razor-wire fence and pressed the buzzer on the gatehouse, a square, stone building under the imposing watch of a gun tower. The officer in the tower controlled all access and was backed-up with a hefty arsenal: a Beretta .40 caliber pistol loaded with twelve rounds and three extra magazines, a Mini-14 rifle loaded with twenty rounds and two extra magazines, an M79 Tear Gas gun that was ready to be loaded at an instant's notice, and a loaded eight-shot Remington 870 12 gauge shotgun, along with an extra box of shells. While he waited for the tower to buzz him in, the Captain's mind wan-dered to LeAnn; on this side of the gatehouse, his mind still belonged fully to him.

LeAnn got good grades and had never been a problem, yet she didn't seem to know what she wanted to do after high school. He and Maura were urging her to live at home and attend a local state college for the first year or two. She'd be paying for part of her college expenses, and this would save them all money. LeAnn didn't seem mature enough to make it on her own yet. She still had a year to go before they had to decide, but a year didn't seem as long as it used to.

The Captain had always said he was grateful that both LeAnn and Marie took after their mother, physically. But sometimes it seemed a curse. At seventeen, LeAnn — five-foot-three-inches and about a hundred and fifteen pounds — was as petite as her mother, though the Captain's Danish side of the family had given her blond hair and blue eyes. She never suffered a shortage of boys interested in her, and it seemed to the Captain that this was a major distraction. About two weeks ago, between boyfriends, she'd received calls from four different boys in the space of half an hour. "Well I could weigh three hundred pounds — no one would call then!'" she said when the Captain complained.

"That sounds good to me," he said, "wanna go get some pie?"

Within a week, she had a new boyfriend. The Captain had quietly "run a check" on him, as he did on all of her boyfriends. This one had an underage drinking citation from two years ago, nothing since. Still, the Captain would keep an eye on him.

Even Marie, his baby, was beginning to look at boys as something other than a nuisance. At thirteen, she was an inch taller than her big sister, with slightly darker blond hair and piercing green eyes. She too, was destined to be a beauty, though braces, baby-fat and an occasional pimple caused her to doubt it. She was going through the awkward stages, one moment content to be mommy's little girl, the next complaining that "everyone treats me like a child." Lately, she and Maura had been clashing, as Maura struggled to hold onto her, and Marie asserted her independence. Often, the Captain felt like a referee. More than once when he interfered, he'd become the target. He had a hard time not getting in the middle, it was such a part of his work life, yet he knew that he had to step away and let them work it out. They were a lot alike, artistic and stubborn. Like her mother, Marie often held a sketch pad when they watched movies; she drew wonderful pictures of the lead characters. But she was more private than LeAnn, and no one outside of the family had seen her artwork.

By the time the tower buzzed him into the gatehouse, a blue-shirt was crossing the parking lot behind him, so the Captain waited, holding the doorwith one hand and the bag of bagels with the other. The officer, Sergeant Tom Warinski, picked up his pace. "Thanks, Cap," Warinski said, as the Captain followed him in. "When are they going to schedule the weapons qualifications?" Sergeant Warinski was the same age as the Captain, a couple of inches shorter, with a full head of thick, dark hair which he wore longer than the current fashion; he was continually brushing it out of his eyes. His smile was contagious, and he was one of the few officers whom the Captain considered a friend. They had worked together as officers for years, and when the Captain was promoted, Warinski had sincerely congratulated him, though Warinski had been the competition. Warinski lived in the village where the Captain worked as a cop, and the Captain had an open invitation to stop for coffee not only in his housing unit at the prison, but at his home when on patrol. The invitation was accepted on more occasions than either man could count.

"I think they'll have us shoot sometime in February," the Captain said, as they lined up at the metal detector. "They don't want to make it too comfortable." It was a standing joke that officers were scheduled for the range when the weather was rotten. It was so cold the last time, they had called themselves the "Tundra Team."

The guardhouse, on the other hand, was cozy — overheated as usual — but that's the way Officer Edna Conley, the skinny, aging, third-shift officer, liked it. She ushered the blue-shirt through the metal detector with an easy smile. "Take it easy, Cap," Warinski called over his shoulder as he headed across the yard toward the administration building to join the other officers in the muster room, where they'd shoot the shit and drink coffee until roll-call.

The Captain removed all the metal he had in his pockets and on his belt, making small talk with Edna. As usual, the metal detector went off the first time he walked through. "Must be the lead in your ass," she chuckled, checking his jacket pockets again. She found a quarter lodged in the crease of the front right pocket. She placed it in the tray with his keys and badge, and he walked through again, this time clearing.

"I'll bet you were hoping for a little wind this morning, huh?" he said as he gathered his equipment.

"Why's that?" Edna said, with a knowing smile.

"I heard with a strong tail wind and a new broom, you can make it home in ten minutes," he said as he walked out of the door. Edna flapped a hand after him in mock disgust.

It was a short walk to the side door of his office in the admin. building, which, besides the shift commanders' offices, housed — all on one floor — the visiting center, medical and clinical services, and offices for the warden and Thorson. There was a small parking lot outside of the supervisor's office, where the cars assigned to the Captain and Lieutenant were parked. No personal cars were allowed in the inner perimeter, but a small fleet of state vehicles, ranging from pick-up trucks to transportation vans, filled the lot. The sun was just starting to rise off to the Captain's left, and the air was as cold and as crisp as a fresh apple. Beyond the perimeter road, hoar frost twinkled on the trees, like the lights in the Crystal Palace. It was going to be a beautiful day.

A few yards away from the open door to the Captain's office, the third shift captain, Harold Schmidt, stood smoking a cigarette and whistling up a storm. That meant either that he had days off ahead or that he'd had a quiet night. Captain Schmidt, at fifty-six, was built like Barney Fife, sinewy and lean. From a distance, he looked like a heavily mustached fourteen-year-old. He was a Black Belt in Judo and ran his own school.

Captain Schmidt didn't notice the Captain approaching, and he jumped at the loud, "'Morning Smitty, rough night?"

Smitty scowled at him, though the curve of his smile gave him away. Exhaling smoke through his nostrils like a huffing bull, he stated. "Not too bad." Only at this range were the signs of age evident. Smitty's hair was pepper-gray, and crows-feet and laugh-lines etched his face. As the lone supervisor on third shift, he was in charge, and the Captain sometimes envied him; neither Smitty nor the Captain took well to petty bureaucrats. Smitty was tough and smart, his only weakness a notoriously delicate stomach. The mere mention of bodily functions caused him to flinch, and the sight of blood was enough to gag him. Stubbing out his cigarette on the stucco wall, he gestured the Captain into their office.

The Captain put the bagels on the desk, pointing for Smitty to help himself, then shrugged off his coat, hung it on the rack in the corner, and sank into a chair at the spare desk, waiting to be briefed.

Smitty sat at the shift commander's desk, bouncing a pencil on its eraser point. "A guy in Unit Three had chest pains, so we sent him to the hospital. Two roommates in Unit Twelve decided they didn't like each other anymore. They're both in segregation. Other than that, it was quiet." He stood up, plucked the daily clipboard off its nail on the wall, scanned it, and replaced it.

"You've got seventeen transfers in, nine transfers out and five releases today. Four counties are coming in to pick up guys for court, and we have five inmates scheduled to go off-grounds for medical appointments." Smitty paced the room, his footsteps a counterpoint to the energetic monolog. The Captain wondered how he could stand the boredom of third shift, but Smitty never seemed bored. "You'll need to get Wilcox, Fourtney and Winslow relieved for grievance hearings at 11:30," Smitty said. "You have two extra officers, so you don't have to pull a patrol to relieve someone." Smitty strode to the wall and peered again at the clipboard. "Oh, yeah, the inmate with the chest pains is back from the hospital. They said he's faking, so he's in medical observation." He plopped back down at the desk, propped his feet on it, and clasped his hands behind his head.

Lieutenant Scott Gaines, the Captain's assistant shift commander, came in through the parking lot door clasping a mug of gas-station coffee in both hands, one long tail of his white shirt hanging out over his rump, the other bunched awkwardly at the belt. His neck tie was about three inches too short and hung off to one side. His overhanging belly partially hid his duty belt, and his pants were so wrinkled it looked like he'd slept in them. Below his shirt pocket, a small coffee stain dribbled beltward. Without a word, the Captain took a "Tide" bleach pen from a desk drawer and threw it to Gaines.

Gaines hung his coat on the rack, muttered "'Mornin'," and, while he scrubbed at the coffee stain with one hand, grabbed the bag of bagels with the other, rummaged one out, and took a bite. He chewed thoughtfully as he picked up the daily clipboard to read what he'd missed. The Captain had reminded Gaines, on more than one occasion, to straighten out his uniform, but the thirty-four-year-old was perpetually rumpled. Given his renewed bachelor status, pressed uniforms and shined boots wouldn't be high on his list of priorities for a while. Despite his appearance, or perhaps because of it, Gaines's skills were often underestimated. One of the best investigators at the prison, he also commanded the Hostage Negotiations Team. He was an expert on street gangs, and because of his non-threatening demeanor, he was a whiz at getting people to open up to him. He had worked alongside Sergeant Murphy in Unit Ten, refining his skills with inmates, until his promotion to lieutenant at the start of the summer.

He was also a pretty good cribbage player; the Captain had written him up twice, when Gaines was still a blue-shirt, for playing cards with an inmate.

"How's the kids?" the Captain said.

"Good." Lt. Gaines popped the last piece of bagel into his mouth. "I just wish I had them for more than a day or two at a time."

The oldest of Gaines's three kids from the first marriage was seven, and they stayed overnight at his house two or three times a week, often overlapping with the toddler from his second marriage. After two marriages gone sour, Gaines was contemplating number three. Though he was short and pudgy, he never had a problem attracting the ladies. He just had a problem keeping them.

The Captain and Smitty helped themselves to bagels, and the three bullshitted a while about life in the prison. While Smitty was wiping a crumb off his shirt, the Captain gave Gaines a slight nod. There were loud footsteps in the hall; it was time to start "the plan."

Officer Chris Harmson knocked at the hallway door and opened it a crack. "C'mon in, Chris," the Captain said. "What can I do for you?"

Officer Harmson, who was in charge of the inmate clean-up crew, stepped in holding a yellow contamination bag at arm's length. "Captain," he said, "you might want to take a look at this. I found it in the inmate bathroom next to the visiting room. You're gonna want to put on some gloves."

Harmson placed the bag gingerly on the floor. Gaines and Smitty looked at it. The Captain put his half-eaten bagel on the desk, stood up, pulled on a pair of rubber gloves, picked-up the bag, and reached into it, extracting what looked like a pair of soiled jockey shorts. He grimaced.

"What is it?" Smitty asked. He took his feet off the desk and stood.

"Oh, man!" Lieutenant Gaines chimed in, jumping up. "Looks like some dude shit his pants!"

Smitty swallowed hard and slowly backed away. The Captain held the shorts to his nose and sniffed, then thrust them out to arms length, wrinkling his nose in disgust. "It's crap, all right." He brought the shorts in, as though to confirm and . . . took a bite!

He chewed loudly, licking his lips. "Fresh crap, too!" He held the dirty underwear out to Smitty as he chewed. "Try some, Smitty, it ain't so bad once you work past the smell."

Smitty kept backing up, his mustache retracted, his face contorted. He hit the wall as he started to gag, his Adam's apple working like a bobber with a fish on the hook.

"The guy had peanuts," the Captain said, taking another bite, working it around with his tongue. Smitty lunged off the wall, pushed past him, and barely made it out the door before he started vomiting. He leaned over a sewer grate, heaving and retching. After a couple of minutes, he straightened up and wiped his mouth on the cuff of his white shirt. Tears streamed down his cheeks. His face was drained of color.

"Want some?" the Captain said, standing in the doorway, holding out the shorts. "Tastes just like a Baby Ruth!"

Smitty's Adam's apple bobbed once, and he started to retch but stopped suddenly and squared his shoulders. "You big bastard! You'll pay for this!" He balled his fists.

Harmson and Gaines crowded behind the Captain, trying to suppress their laughter. Then Gaines pushed past, pretending to gag, leaning over the grate. Smitty, despite himself, issued a plaintive cry, and retched again. When Smitty subsided, Gaines was doubled up with laughter, and Harmson was stumbling out into the parking lot, his eyes streaming with tears.

Smitty glared at the Captain. "You big son-of-a-bitch! I hate you." If he hadn't been smiling — breaking into chuckles — the Captain might have believed him.

"How'd you set it up?" Smitty asked after he'd cleaned himself up and they were settling back into the office.

Harmson had taken a pair of new inmate underwear, the Captain explained, and inserted a Baby Ruth candy bar in the crotch, then melted it in a microwave.

"I hate you," Smitty repeated, laughing. "I'll make it my life's work to pay you back."

The Captain gave him a pat on the back as he brushed past, grabbing the first-shift officer roster. "I'll take the muster room."

Usually, lieutenants took roll in the muster room, but on first watch, the Captain did it himself. There was no need for a mass briefing, no major drama to deal with today, just the checklist of each officer's scheduled assignment. Though each officer has an assigned post and worked the same post every day, it was up to the supervisors to make sure they were there. He walked down the hallway and from twenty feet away, he could hear the conversation and laughter. He entered the room and as the talked dyed-off, he began: "Sergeant Murphy, Unit Ten." The Captain ticked off his name.

Murphy was his usual spit and polish, and though clothes didn't always make the man, his care in dressing reminded the Captain that Murph could be counted on if the shit hit the fan.

"Sergeant Warinski, Unit Eight. Let's try to keep the roof on today, Tom, OK?" A newspaper poked out of the inside pocket of Warinski's uniform jacket. Though staff weren't supposed to read on duty, the Captain knew it helped cut the boredom of the day. It was the most widely ignored rule in the institution, as long as the officers didn't flaunt it, as long as they put down whatever they were reading when a supervisor came into their unit.

Warinski smiled his easy smile, tipped his hat and said, "I'll do the state proud."

"Sgt. King, Unit seven." A gruff looking, forty-year-old with the build of a stevedore stepped forward. "'Morning Al," the Captain said, "how were the days off" Too fucken' short," came the response, as gruff as the man that issued it."I'll bet you wife is glad they're over, though?" the Captain retorted, earning a smile from King.

"Officer Winslow, Tower Six." Karl Winslow was a short man who hid his paunch under a dark blue sweater or vest, no matter the time of year or temperature. At thirty-five-years-old, Winslow was already at the pinnacle of his career. He wanted to do nothing more than spend the next 20 years sitting in a tower, eating bologna sandwiches, listening to the radio, and complaining how rough life was. He still lived with his parents and, except for a car payment, had no bills. The Captain only hoped Winslow would stay awake until his grievance hearing.

There were sixty-five officers and sergeants on first shift, and like the cons, ninety percent were there to do a job. The other ten percent were a royal pain in the ass, pissing and moaning about perceived discrepancies with the union contract, worried that

NO PLACE LIKE HOME

they weren't getting their share of overtime. That was Winslow's class.

He had filed a grievance against the Captain because the Captain had missed his name on an overtime sign-up sheet. Winslow had never accepted overtime, but took the chance for some free money. When an Officer won an overtime grievance, he didn't have to make up the time but simply received eight hours pay at time-and-a-half. He'd probably win the grievance. Personnel would be mad, but fuck 'em. Maybe if they came up with a workable policy and didn't expect supervisors to drop everything to make overtime calls, vultures like Winslow would have nothing to cry about.

"Sergeant Andrea Golden, Unit Sixteen." Ass-hats like Golden were another matter. They'd always have something to cry about because they never could shake the idea that the inmates were the enemy. Come to think of it, it wasn't just inmates: everybody seemed to be Golden's enemy. She barely nodded to acknowledge her assignment, a barracks that housed close to one-hundred-fifty unlucky inmates.

"Sgt. Dixon, unit fourteen, seg." the Captain said as he checked the name off of the roster. "Don't let them push your buttons today, Ted," the Captain advised, an inside joke because Dixon hated anyone pressing the door buzzers in seg.

"Officer Cunningham, Administration Security." The Captain would keep an eye on Michelle Cunningham today. She was having a hard time with her soon-to-be ex-husband. Thorson had bitched her out yesterday for having "her head up her ass," after she'd allowed an unescorted inmate to step into the infirmary, and a nurse had complained. Never mind that there was an officer already back there, it was Cunningham's job to make sure that all inmates had an escort into and out of the infirmary, and she'd let a guy go back by himself.

The mistake was really no big security risk, but Cunningham had screwed-up. It was just another excuse for Thorson to throw his weight around.

The Captain had stood up for Cunningham, mentioning the nasty divorce, and the little prick had responded with his usual arrogance. "I don't give a shit. If she can't do her job, she needs to go home." Cunningham was a good officer, but the stress was telling on her, and Thorson would have no mercy if she messed up again. The Captain would back her up all he could for a while. It didn't help that she was stationed right across from Thorson's office. But maybe even Cunningham would catch a break. Maybe it would be a quiet day.

The officers continued to stream in and check in for their assignments. One of the last to come was Dave Wilkins.

"Wilkins, Security Patrol" the Captain said as Wilkins walked by. Glancing up, the Captain saw the blood-shot eyes. "Rough night?" the Captain asked.

"No worse than usual." Wilkins shrugged.

"Great," thought the Captain, "another hangover." Wilkins was his right-hand man among the blue shirts; a moody headache would make him a difficult partner.

CHAPTER II

The "Code One" came as the Captain was breaking his own rule, allowing his mind to wonder outside of the fence. He'd been thinking about LeAnn's piano recital from two days ago, how beautifully she had played Beethoven's "Fur Elise." His mind was replaying the haunting melody when the blare of the radio on his belt broadcast the "Code One," bringing him harshly back to the present. A "Code One" meant that the shit was hitting the fan somewhere. It was either a fight, an assault, or someone seriously hurt, be it staff or inmate.

They were only a short ways down the road, and Wilkins pressed the gas pedal closer to the floor. The van leapt forward and screeched to a stop by the end of the square concrete barracks unit. By plan, the Captain jumped out and ran to the front door, directing Wilkins to go in through a side door to the kitchen area, where he'd be able to see the dayroom and commons areas. From inside the front door, the Captain could see the inmate bunk area, but — at first — no inmates. It was quiet in the whole dorm, but it was the type of quiet that caused the hair on the back of his neck to rise. It was the type of quiet that one felt before a tornado — the type the Captain feared more than the thought of his own death. In the brief millisecond that it took to scope the unit for signs of a disturbance, every fiber of the Captain's being told him that something was seriously wrong. It wasn't until the Captain turned the corner into the dining area that his gaze reached the huge group inmates — maybe sixty – in the gloom at the far corner of the room. The majority were black, with a few "wannabes" in the mix. They were all looking toward Wilkins, whose footsteps they could hear coming through the kitchen.

At that moment, the Captain realized he was no longer in control of his life. At that moment, he knew what he had to do.

* * *

7:30am

THE CAPTAIN MADE HIS WAY down the hallway and went into the secured Control Center. It was time for the first count. Official count was taken six times a day, with the first at 7; 39. Morning count required that every inmate in the prison — all seventeen hundred of them — stand by his cell doorway and be physically counted by the unit officer. The units were locked down for the fifteen or so minutes it would take for the count to "clear." The numbers were called in to the Captain, who cross-checked and verified each unit's count status, making sure each inmate was where he was supposed to be.

As soon he'd cleared the count, the Captain left the secure control center and walked down the hallway to his office. A lot of the "pretty people" — the eight to four, Monday to Friday crowd — were starting to come in, non-security staff that had their own supervisors. Ultimately, in theory anyway, security was the foremost priority for everyone, even the pretty people. But they seemed to come from a different planet — a planet the Captain admired. A planet where they were free from the danger, a planet where numbers and shuffling papers was more important, a planet removed from the reality of what happened behind the locked cell doors, a planet where they were free from the human wreckage of inmates,

As he passed the inmate records office, he spotted Lisa, the records clerk secretary. She had freckles on her broad cheeks and curls that bounced when she turned, and she was always, unaccountably, cheerful. Lisa was barely older than LeAnn and had finished her degree at a community college. A typical country girl, she still lived with her parents on the family farm. "Mornin',

Lisa," the Captain chimed, happy to see a smiling face. "Ready to give your all for the state?"

"Just like every day!" Lisa said with a laugh, shaking her head, her hair swinging.

The Captain continued to his office, where Thorson was sitting at the spare desk, a pile of yesterday's reports on each side of him. He pointed at a couple that he had set in front of him. "Captain," he said, way too loudly, "these reports need to be rewritten. I don't know how many times I have to tell these fucktards not to use blue ink on reports."

The Captain shrugged. Thorson was notoriously foulmouthed, and altered his vocabulary only in the presence of superiors.

Thorson cocked a thumb at the Captain's computer screen. The Captain had changed his screensaver to read, "PROFANITY IS AN AUDIBLE EXPRESSION OF IGNORANCE."
"What the fuck does that mean?" Thorson roared.

Ignoring Thorson, but smiling to himself at the irony, the Captain lifted his radio shoulder mic and started to transmit a call. Often, the best strategy, he'd found, was simply to continue doing his job, as though Thorson weren't there. Thorson liked to rip everything and everyone apart, but even there, he had a limited attention span. Just as the Captain had hoped, Thorson spun around and headed out of the room.

"Oak eighteen," the Captain said, "to Oak seventy-one."

"Oak seventy-one," came the reply.

"Oak seventy-one, report to the security office for staff transport."

"Ten-four, I'm en route."

Captains and lieutenants on most shifts rode in their own vehicles, but not on first shift. Both the Captain and Lieutenant Gaines made their rounds with patrol officers. It kept them in the trenches, and made them part of a team. The blue-shirts on first shift trusted that, if anything came up, the white-shirts would be there, in the midst of the ruckus, to help. Many times, either the Captain or Gaines had jumped into the fray, physically restraining inmates, handcuffing them, and escorting them to segregation. Just last week, the Captain had taken a couple of cheap shots to the jaw when he'd tackled an inmate who had struck Officer Wilkins.

It would take Officer Wilkins a couple of minutes to come fetch him, so the Captain grabbed a twenty-four ounce bottle of diet Coke out of the small refrigerator that sat between the desks. Diet Coke was his only vice. He'd taken up the habit when he'd quit smoking, and a couple of years after that, he'd quit drinking, so, for the most part, diet Coke was his surrogate for both smokes and booze. He was rarely seen without a bottle of the fizzy stuff within grabbing distance. He really liked the damned stuff.

He put his coat on, picked up his bottle, and went out to the parking lot to wait. Sipping at the Coke, he took in the quiet of the day, soaked up the peace of sunshine and woods. In five minutes, inmate movement would be allowed to resume, and any reverie of nature would be shattered, even by the simplest of routines. A dark blue mini-van appeared on the road and pulled up beside him.

"So," Officer Wilkins said, "I get to be C.B. for the morning. "C.B." was short for "Captain's Bitch," a name the patrols had christened themselves when the Captain started riding with them. At thirty-one, Dave Wilkins had a calm, humble style and a direct, reassuring gaze. He was shorter than the Captain by a few inches, with straight brown hair and intense blue eyes. His wife, Cindy, was four months pregnant, but Wilkins was a private man, and the Captain was pretty sure that nobody else at work knew.

Wilkins had confided in the Captain long ago that his sister had been murdered, at nineteen — when he was sixteen. She had gone out one night to meet friends, and someone had stabbed her in the parking lot of a dance club. She'd bled to death before the ambulance got there. They never caught the murderer. All they knew, from a witness, was that he was young and black.

A few months after his sister's death, Wilkins had found his mother's body hanging from a rafter in the garage. His father had escaped into the comfort of a bottle.

The Captain had once asked Wilkins if he ever wondered whether one of the inmates might be the guy who did it. "I used to wonder that all of the time, when I first started," Dave said, "but I realized that if I was going to brood on it, I was in the wrong business. I'm not a religious man, but I know that some-day, the guy's going to have to pay, one way or another."

The Captain and Wilkins never spoke of it again.

Wilkins had been with Corrections — and at North Woods— for almost ten years, and he knew everyone on the place. He commanded a six-man squad on Lieutenant Gaines's Institution Hostage Negotiations Team and had recently been appointed chief hostage negotiator. If the team were ever needed, he would be the first man on the phone. Gaines was in charge, but there were no negotiators over the rank of Sergeant that con-ducted actual negotiations. That way, the person on the phone was a stop-gap, because he couldn't give then anything. It helped create an "us versus them" mentality between the negotiator and the inmate: both sides were dependent on someone else to make the final decision. Officer Dave Wilkins had shown his skills many times, most recently when he had freed a cook held at knife-point in the main kitchen. Wilkins was already on a first-name basis with the inmate perpetrator, and after talking with Wilkins for an hour, the man simply dropped the knife and released the kitchen worker.

The Captain didn't mind trusting his life to Wilkins; more than once, they had backed each other up in a fight. Once, when they were locking a man up for being disruptive and the Captain was droning through his usual speech about cooperating, the inmate, without warning, thrust his hand into his right pocket. The Captain grabbed his arm above the wrist and made him kiss concrete — a vertical stun — forcing him hard into the wall. Wilkins grabbed the inmate's left hand, and they threw him to the floor and cuffed him. "I was just reaching for my Carmex," the inmate panted, and when they searched him, sure enough, they found the Carmex in his right pocket.

For a long time, Wilkins teased the Captain. "Watch out! This one might have Chapstick!" The Captain knew, though, that the officers and blue-shirts liked his approach and followed it — the specific, routine instructions that let an inmate know what was safe to do and what wasn't. It generally worked: the inmates taught newcomers not to reach into their pockets unless they wanted to kiss concrete.

As Wilkins steered the Dodge mini-van along the south side of Unit Nine, the low sunlight glinted on the windows of the cell-block — almost like stained glass, the Captain thought. Sometimes the beauty of a fall day seeped in, even to a world defined by razor wire and gun towers. They passed a dark blue van coming the other direction, patrolling the roads. Lieutenant Gaines waved from the driver's seat.

"How's Dern?" Wilkins said. "How's he doing in Unit Fifteen?" Dern was a new officer whom Wilkins had been assigned to train.

"He came around," Gaines said, rolling to a stop. "It just took him a while to get his head on straight. I think you straightened it out for him."

"Sure," Wilkins said, wheeling the van through a turn-around in front of Unit Five and pulling to a stop next to Gaines.

"You still showing that picture?" the Captain asked Wilkins.

"I got it," Wilkins said, digging in his wallet and pulling out a dog-eared photo. The Captain took it — a black kid about 2-years-old sitting on the floor dressed like a conductor and playing with a toy train. "He'll be graduating in another couple of years," Wilkins said. "He's real good in math. Still mows my lawn."

The Captain chuckled. The kid in the photo was Wilkins's neighbor, but when Wilkins had been a Field Training Officer, partnering with officers fresh from the academy for three weeks, he used to take it out whenever people started talking about their kids. "Looks just like his mother," Wilkins would say. "Fine boy," and he'd watch their reaction.

Gary Dern was an ex-Marine who, as a rookie, often made racist comments. It was more from ignorance, Wilkins had suggested to the Captain, than from malice. Dern had grown up, as had many of the officers, in a small town that offered him little or no exposure to people of different races or cultures. His parents had taught him some real stupidities, Wilkins figured, and his friends in the Corps — where he was exposed to minorities for the first time — had only made things worse. "Give him some rope," the Captain had said. "Let's see what he does."

One afternoon, after Wilkins and Dern had helped Lieutenant Gaines lock up a black inmate, Dern had started mouthing off. "Man," he said, flapping a hand in front of his nose, "that was one smelly Coon."

Wilkins just smiled. "Let me show you something," he said, reaching for his wallet. He handed Dern the photo. "My son makes a fine train conductor, don't you think?"

The color drained from Dern's face, as he handed it back. "Now, what were you saying about Coons?" Wilkins smiled. "Why don't we go talk to the Captain, and you can tell him all about Coons, and while you're at it, you can tell him about Mexicans and Indians and Asians. I forget all the proper names for those." He smoothed the picture with his thumb and slipped it back into his wallet.

"I didn't mean anything by it," Dern blurted. "I was just talkin'.

Wilkins never raised his voice, but fixed his intense blue eyes on the stocky Marine. "Talk like that will get you fired if the Captain hears it, and killed if an inmate hears it. In here, it doesn't matter what color someone is." He dropped his voice to a whisper, still smiling. "They are here to do their time, not put up with ignorant-ass comments about Coons or Spics or Crackers."

Dern hung his head and nodded, muttering, "I'm an idiot."

"No disagreeing on that point. I'll tell you what," Wilkins said, "you've got two more weeks with me to clean up your act. If I hear anymore crap out of you, I'm turning you in. Do you understand me?" he whispered. "That shit has to stop." He walked away, and Dern followed, a chastised child, head hanging. The Captain heard the whole exchange from inside the officer's station and knew that Wilkins had handled it properly.

Dern's career hinged on Wilkins's training and recommendations, but the Captain knew that wasn't the only thing that changed him. Once he cleaned up his talk, he started to look at the inmates as people, instead of inferior races to be put down or laughed at. Dern made it through probation fine. He became a decent, cool-headed officer, working in the treatment unit, the largest in the institution. He seemed to have put his prejudices behind him.

Wilkins had, at most, a high school diploma, yet he could read people — officers or inmates — better than most shrinks. He had probably been exposed to more varied and profound mental quirks in his ten years at North Woods than most psychologists encounter in a career, and he paid attention. He was what people in another environment might have called intuitive.

The three complexes of housing units all met at a common intersection and the Captain expected all four of his mobile patrols to be parked at the intersection during times of mass movement — when the inmates were on their way to or from the school and the maintenance complex. He and Wilkins followed Gaines over to park at the intersection, and they all got out to watch and maybe help with pat-down searches. Usually the pat downs were conducted at random. Sometimes a whole unit would be searched. The inmates were accustomed to it.

Officer Nathaniel Walters, a short black officer, patted down a black inmate who loomed over him. "Man," he said, "I'm going to have to do a 'chalk and pat' on you, you're so big."

"What's that?" the inmate asked.

"Well," Walters explained, "I take a piece of chalk and mark where I left off so I know where to start up again!" An elderly inmate laughed, and Walters said sternly, "Quit laughing! You're in prison. You ain't supposed to have fun!" But he was smiling.

"It looks like you're having a little too much fun, pattin' on Big O that way!" The elderly inmate said, and Walters and Big O laughed.

"Man," Big O told Walters, "you just ain't right!" Shaking his head and grinning, Big O lumbered off to school.

The Captain was under no illusion that there wasn't contraband around. There was always pot, and a few shanks, but most inmates weren't stupid enough to carry them. They usually stashed them in common areas, so if officers found them, there was no proof as to whom they belonged. Most of the shanks inmates made were for protection from other inmates, but not always.

The first time the Captain was attacked with a shank was when he was a sergeant in Unit One in the early eighties, after the big influx of Cuban inmates. Rene Herrera was a little guy, about five-foot three-inches and maybe, soaking wet, a hundred pounds. But there wasn't an ounce of fat on his body; he was all muscle and sinew, with jet black hair, fierce black eyes, and pearl white teeth. Shortly after Rene came into the unit, he started calling the hefty blond Captain — his physical opposite — "Pa." The Cuban was twenty years old, and the Captain, at the time, only twenty-five, hardly old enough to be his father. Yet, Rene insisted on calling him "Pa."

"Pa," he'd say when he came into the Captain's office, "how come ju workin' in des place? Peoples here es no goo." It made the Captain chuckle. When he asked Rene why he called him Pa, Rene said, "I neber had no Pa. Ju take care of me like a Pa. Ju make sure I get food. If I get sick, ju send me to nurse, and ju don' let no one hurt me. Ju just like a Pa."

Rene had been sent to prison for stabbing someone in a fight. All he said about it was, "Pa, he tried to hurt me, so I stabbed heem. I din' keel heem doe, I just stabbed heem a leetle beet."

Around the time Rene came, a couple of young white inmates were making known their dislike of blacks. The head of the white faction, Brian Augustine, was a nineteen-year-old from a farming community who had quit school when he turned sixteen. Augustine had the muscular build of a farm hand, and he had never met a black man until he came to prison. Kenny Reeves, also about nineteen — six-foot two and as skinny as a rail — headed the black faction. Reeves was as overtly racist against whites as any member of the KKK against blacks. Between these two, there was no love lost.

One day when the Captain was "standing the food line" — monitoring lunch — a commotion erupted at the back of the dining hall. The Captain ran back in time to see Augustine cold cock Reeves. As Reeves went down, Augustine started to pummel him.

The Captain punched his body alarm and tackled Augustine, knocking him off Reeves. Augustine wrapped his arms around the Captain, and as they tumbled, inmates scattered from their tables, overturning food trays. Augustine was stronger, but the Captain still had the agility of the wrestler he had been in high school. He maneuvered behind Augustine, got him in a choke hold, and could feel the inmate starting to lose consciousness when from behind him, a scream erupted.

More like a high-pitched howl, really: It was Rene, who had started from a table near the windows in pursuit of Reeves, who had produced a six-inch-long shank and was running at the Captain. The little Cuban seemed to fly over the tables, launching himself onto Reeves's back, wrapping his legs around the tall man's waist, and clawing at his face with both hands. "Ju motherfuck!" he yelled, "Ju don' hurt my Pa!" The tall man dropped the knife and grabbed for Rene, who clung to him like a spider monkey, tearing at his face. The two of them spun around the dining area, a cyclone of rage and flailing arms. The shank clattered to the floor, and an inmate kicked it to the Captain, as he rose from cuffing the semi-conscious Augustine. Other inmates grabbed Reeves and pried Rene off of him.

The little Cuban bounded over to the captain, hiked up his green inmate pants, and assumed a boxer's crouch, facing the crowd of inmates. "Don ju worry, Pa, I cover ju back."

Teeth marks on Reeves's right hand later showed it must have been Rene's bite that loosened the shank. But Rene was hardly around long enough to receive the Captain's thanks. Five days after the incident, one of Augustine's friends threatened him at school, and the Cuban stabbed him with a ballpoint pen — not enough to kill him — "just a leetle beet" — but plenty to get Rene transferred to Maximum Security at another prison, one hundred miles north.

The Captain never saw him again.

The Captain watched Walters and the other blue-shirts chatting with the inmates as they filed past, impressed, as always, with the rapport. Inmates and blue-shirts joked and talked with obvious respect. That wasn't a gimme in a place like North Wood; good relations flowed like a stream in the forest from officer to blue-shirt to inmate, and the Captain consciously tended to the flow every day, modeling encouraging behavior, imbuing trainees with dignity and decency, and rewarding a light-hearted attitude as a reminder that life could be good, even in the joint.

The pat searches were turning up nothing big today: a couple of cigarettes, a borrowed magazine. But toward the end of the line, one inmate stood out. He was young, perhaps nineteen, tall and spindly. Defiance tightened his face, and he was visibly nervous as Lt. Gaines and Officer Sandy Hoover, a slight twenty-nine year-old with sandy blond hair, approached to search him. He turned to walk away.

"Say, fella," Lt. Gaines said as he consciously tugged his pants over his pot-belly, "you need to come over here."

The inmate turned his head but kept walking, and his reply was the sound of air leaking out a tire. "Pssssh."

"Dude," Lt. Gaines said, louder. "You best stop your ass right now! One more step and you're going to the hole."

The inmate took a couple of more steps, but Lt. Gaines, Officer Hoover, Walters and Wilkins already had him surrounded.

"Hold up for a minute," the Captain called, raising an arm, and the long file of inmates heading for the big brick building stopped moving. The few inmates who remained to be searched stood in a tight line next to the road. "You guys," the Captain directed those on the way to the school, "Turn toward the school. There's nothing to see back here. You other guys, look the other way." It wasn't that he didn't want witnesses; rather, he didn't want anyone else to join in.

Lt. Gaines studied the ID card dangling on the chest of the angry young inmate. "So, Stanley Burroughs, what's your problem?" he said. "All we were going to do is search you and send you to school." Hoover and Walters moved to either side of the inmate, and Wilkins closed in directly behind him.

"Man," the inmate replied, "I ain't lettin' no one put their hand up by my junk, and this little bitch ain't touchin' me neither."

As the inmate spoke, Lt. Gaines nodded a slight "yes", and the officers sprung into action. Hoover and Walters grabbed him by the wrist and elbow and cranked his arms behind him. Wilkins snapped cuffs over his wrists.

The inmate stood blinking, as though surprised that they hadn't given him time to land a punch or to explain himself further.

"That was just pure stupid," Lt. Gaines said. "Officer Hoover, pat him down."

Hoover had worked as an officer since she was nineteen, and because she was young and pretty, with a nice figure and an out-going personality, inmates often wrongly assumed her to be an "easy mark." The fact was, she knew her job and wasn't afraid to do it. "Sir," she asked Burroughs as she approached, "is there anything in your pockets that might stab or hurt either of us?" He shook his head. She started the search at his collar line, running her fingers around the inside, then swiping her hands down each arm, the front of his chest and the small of his back, keeping her hands in contact as she patted the sides of his upper torso. She had him lift each foot for a patting, then ran her hands up his leg. When she got to his crotch, she used the edge of her hands to explore the area next to "his junk." He tensed, but stood still. She moved on to his rear, and in the back pocket of his pants, found a small, tightly folded piece of paper.

The Captain peered over her shoulder as she opened it: a pretty good line drawing of a naked man.

Looking into the eyes of the glowing red Burroughs, Officer Hoover asked, "Is this what this is about?"

He nodded, looking at his feet like a chastised child.

Lt. Gaines stepped forward and took the scrap of paper. He shook his head sadly. "If this is all you had, you'd have been written up for contraband. Now, you're going to the hole." Lt. Gaines nodded toward the patrol van and took his place opposite Walters, at Burroughs's elbow. "I'll let you make a statement when we get there. Let's go." They loaded him up, Officer Hoover climbed into the driver's seat, and as Walters returned to the roll call, she and Lt. Gaines rolled off toward the seg. building with the inmate artist.

"All right, you guys," the Captain told the rest of the inmates. "If you had anything, I sure hope you were smart enough to drop it while that was going on!" The inmates smiled and shook their heads, but the Captain noted a few additional cigarettes and odd papers along the road. "Line up, and let's get this done!"

Walters made the final count of the day's illicit treasures: "I have three skin magazines, found in a bag that no one would claim. I have two packs of cigarettes that I took off of a couple guys. I have their names and told them they'd be getting tickets later for possessing contraband. That's about it. I checked the stuff by the road: three cigarettes and a couple of porn pictures that I just threw away."

Walters sauntered back to his big Dodge patrol van. When he turned the key, the "Thump" of bass from the rap music on the radio drowned out the engine — and just about everything else. Walters smiled, gave a short wave and drove away, his head bobbing to the beat. It wasn't exactly great policy to listen to music so loud that an explosion in a barracks would sound like nothing more than syncopation, but morale and safety were a balancing act: Walters needed his music, and a lot of the inmates connected to him because he knew the gritty, tough, dark lyrics of Dogg Pound and Busta Rhymes and Method Man.

The inmates shuffled off to their classes and jobs, and the Captain and Wilkins climbed in their van to make the rounds of the housing units. Most of the twelve older units had been built on a single floor. At the center, a sergeant's plexi-glass office overlooked the inmate's day room, dining, and recreation area. Cellblocks stretched out to both sides of the office, and the inmate showers stood to the rear. The units had been built to house twenty-five juveniles; now they housed sixty-six adults, two inmates sleeping in each cell and sixteen more on bunk beds in the dayroom.

Contrary to the movies and TV, unit sergeants had only body alarms for protection — no weapons, other than their skills at dealing with inmates. With the odds sixty-six to one against them, most sergeants forgot all the macho crap they'd learned as adolescents and figured out how to talk to people. It was a matter of survival. Most became downright eloquent in their first weeks as trainees — except for the Terminators.

Wilkins had barely turned the key in the ignition when a call crackled over the radio, a "Code Two" to Unit Sixteen, the barracks assigned that morning to Sergeant Andrea Golden. A Code Two wasn't an immediate emergency, so they circled south behind the school building and cruised slowly up along the housing units so as not to raise the anxiety levels of anyone who might be watching. They weren't in any hurry to encounter Sergeant Golden. In her early fifties, she'd been at North Woods as long as the Captain and should have been one of his best assets. But Golden was a "Terminator."

Terminators, in the Captain's lexicon, were officers who strutted around the units like God's gift to Corrections. They liked to think they were setting the standard, doing the job right, while others simply "went through the motions." They never asked themselves why they had more problems than other officers. But while others did what needed to be done — using judgment to enforce the rules fairly — Terminators stood braced and bristling for a challenge to their authority.

Most of them simply weren't cut out for Corrections — there was no way they'd learn — but they hung on, making the days long and life hard on everyone. Of all the assaults the Captain had seen, most had happened when a Terminator was on duty. Often the victim wasn't the Terminator but rather the poor hapless officer who responded, entering the unit without knowing what was going on and confronting a con so mad at the Terminator that he was ready to take on all comers. When the

Captain came upon such a stand-off, the first thing he did, if possible, was to send the Terminator to the office to keep a bad situation from billowing into a full-on horror show.

Sgt. Golden wasn't a regular in any unit but a utility sergeant, taking the place of whoever called in sick or went on vacation. She was like Pigpen in Peanuts, only the cloud she trailed was of write-ups and altercations — usually minor ones, but a pain in the ass for all involved. It wasn't unusual for her to write six or seven conduct reports in a single shift. She treated the inmates like recalcitrant children, and they obliged her by living up to her image of them.

For a while, it was Sgt. Golden's contention that inmates were stalking her. Every day, the Captain or Lieutenant Gaines would get a call complaining that "inmate so-and-so is lying on his bed, and every time I go by his cell, he is looking at me." Or: "Inmate so-and-so walked to the shower in his underwear, and when he looked at me, he had an erection."

The Captain explained, time and again, "Of course they look at you. They're inmates, and you're a woman. Just because an inmate looks at you when you walk by his cell doesn't mean that he's stalking you. They look at me when I walk by, and even if they're gay, it doesn't mean they want me."

"Well," Sergeant Golden snapped, time and again, "I know how they are looking at me, and it's more than just watching!"

Lately, Golden's problem was with the inmate's work. In every unit, she made it a point to find fault with a kitchen worker or swamper. Inevitably, the regular unit sergeants were to blame. "I don't know why the regulars hire such lazy workers," she'd say. "You can't get them to do anything without ordering them."

Wilkins pulled up to the front door of Golden's Unit 16, the barracks, and the Captain sat a moment, eying the square, gray, concrete-block building, the ugliest of the institution, built in a hasty attempt to address overcrowding. The rest of the buildings, the "old units" were constructed out of expertly mortared brick, with pitched roofs and large widows in the dayroom, giving view beyond the fences and razor wire of the beauty of a state forest. The barracks, though had a spartan aspect that was entirely out of place in the scenic beauty of the woods. Unit 16 was a square, squat building made of reinforced concrete block. It's only windows were in the unit managers office and the social workers office, along with long rectangular windows along the roof line every twenty feet. It was, frankly ominous. The Captain heaved himself off the Dodges' sagging seat, ducking his head to keep from scraping it, and followed Wilkins in the front door.

The sergeant's station was as dispiriting as the outside the building. It was on a raised concrete floor, about three feet higher than the living areas. It gave a vantage point to the front entrance and two of the bunk areas. It wasn't a closed secure area, and besides the sergeants desk and telephone, and a waist high counter in the front, and windows into the shower/bathroom area there was little there. The two unit officer sat at desks further back in the bunk areas, monitoring them. The desks they had were basically old metal school teacher's desks, each with a phone on them. There were no barriers between them and the 100 inmates housed on each respective side of the unit.

Sergeant Golden sat at her desk, her hands crossed over her ample chest, fuming. She had short blond hair and regular features. From the waist up, she looked pretty much like your average mean aunt. Before the Captain could even utter a "Good Morning," Sgt. Golden began: "I want him locked up for taking too much sugar," she said, banging a fist on the desk and rising to reveal hips that would put Rosie O'Donnell to shame.

"Who?" the Captain said, motioning her to sit back down and seating himself on a folding chair at the counter next to her desk. Wilkins put a fist to his mouth and cleared his throat to cover a smile.

"Every time I work this unit, Dunbar tries to take two spoons full of sugar in his cereal," she said. Even seated, the Captain mused, she was frightful. Her stiff, bleached hair stood out from her head in little spikes, as though she'd plugged a finger into a socket and the current was coursing through her. "He knows he's only allowed one for coffee and one for cereal, but he tries to take two for his cereal. I told him last time that if he did it again, I'd call a white-shirt. He did it again this morning. I saw him get ready to put another spoonful in his cereal and I stopped him. Then he laughed at me!"

The Captain called Tywan Dunbar into the office. A tall, skinny black man in his early thirties, Dunbar stood out because he had no tattoos — nothing to show that he belonged to a gang — just smooth, coffee-colored arms.

"Good morning, Suh," he greeted the Captain, nodding at Wilkins. He ignored the electric-shock victim across the desk.

"Good Morning." The Captain stood and took measure of Dunbar. He saw a man that looked out of place. He saw a man that was a manipulator. He appeared to be harmless, but he had recently been sent to prison as a serial rapist, and several of his victims had never been found. "The sergeant tells me that you tried to take too much sugar, and when she told you not to, you laughed at her. Is that right?"

Dunbar looked at the floor. "Cap, I din't drink coffee, so I likes to put two spoons of sugar in my cereal." He shook his head apologetically. "I tried to tell Sergeant Golden that, but she just kept yelling at me and wasn't letting me explain. I tried to ax if it was OK, but she just kept yelling. I just smiled at her and said, 'OK, Miss Golden,' and I left the food line."

"Is that what happened?" The Captain turned to Sgt. Golden, who swiveled her creaking chair to face three-quarters away from them, a pouting child refusing to make eye contact.

"The rules say, 'one spoonful for coffee and one for cereal.'" She enunciated each word as though reading from the book. "*Not* two for his cereal!"

The Captain sighed. "Sergeant Golden, what does it matter if he takes two spoonfuls in his cereal? He doesn't drink coffee, and he's not getting any more than any other inmate."

"The rules say . . . " She spun the chair around and faced him, her face red, the veins on her neck throbbing, her blond hair bristling. ". . . one spoonful for coffee, one spoonful for cereal."

"Sergeant Golden, I know what the rules say." The Captain leaned on the counter and brought his face close to hers, sideways. "I also know that the rules can be interpreted differently by different people. My interpretation is that he gets two spoonfuls of sugar for breakfast. I don't care if he puts them in his coffee, on his cereal, in his orange juice, or eats them straight. He gets two spoonfuls of sugar!"

"So, I guess my authority means nothing!" she shot back. "If he can refuse my order in front of forty-five other inmates, I might as well not be here!"

The Captain wished she weren't. He watched her balefully, a cartoon image of frustration, steam shooting from her ears. She was a hot-head, all right, as angry as any con he could think of at the moment. He stood, leaned on the counter, and gazed out the window on the quiet dining room, where a kitchen worker was neatly refilling napkin holders and salt and pepper shakers.

"He didn't refuse your order," he said finally. "Your authority allows you to enforce rules. It doesn't allow you to make them up. I don't see any security risk from Dunbar putting two spoonfuls of sugar on his cereal." He glanced at Dunbar, who stood with his head bowed and his hands clasped loosely at his belly, as though in church.

"I suppose they can get away with just about anything then," Sergeant Golden said. "If I can't get someone locked up for disobeying an order, what can I get them locked up for?"

The Captain sat down and clasped his hands on the counter top, looking Golden in the eye. "I'll place a man in lock-up if he's a danger to himself or others — or a threat to the security of the institution. I *won't* put a man in T.L.U. because he put two spoons of sugar on his cereal!" He turned to Dunbar. "If this sergeant calls me again today and mentions that you are giving her a hard time, I'll lock you up. Do you understand?"

"Yes, Captain. I understand. Don't worry, I ain't gonna give Miss Golden no hard time."

"Sergeant Golden," the Captain said, "if you see Dunbar talking about this with anyone and they give you any trouble, let me know."

"Well, for all the good it'll do," she sniffed. But the fire had gone out of her. She'd probably be all right until the next penny-ante flare-up.

"Boy, she's a piece of work, isn't she?" Wilkins said, as they made their way back to the van.

*   *   *

CHAPTER III

Wilkins emerged from the kitchen and stopped short at the sight of the huge inmate crowd. A black man the Captain recognized as an inmate that just came got off the bus a few hours ago emerged from the crowd. He recognized the scarred, disfigured face of Leon Nelson. He was apparently in control as he pointed a mop handle at Wilkins. "Get that Motherfucker!" he screamed. The door hadn't yet swung closed behind the Captain — and it occurred to him that he could, physically, step back outside, lock the door, and radio for help. But, to him, it wasn't an option, because he wasn't just a man in a body; he was a node in a network. His people depended on him as much as he depended on them. From the corner of his eye, he was aware of a last glimmer of sunlight as the door slammed shut with a steel-and-concrete thud, sealing him into the steel-and-concrete barracks.

"Hey!" the Captain yelled as the crowd started toward Wilkins, "What the hell is the problem here?" The confused inmates stopped and, as a group, turned. Leon pointed at the Captain.

"That's the Motherfucker we want!" They surged away from Wilkins and toward the Captain. By instinct rather than thought, Wilkins ran after them.

"Dave, get out!" the Captain yelled. It was crucial that Wilkins retreat and give the inmates one less hostage. But Wilkins's first instinct was to help, to fight alongside the Captain; he kept coming. "Wilkins! Get the fuck out!"

Wilkins stopped. The obscenity made it a command; the Captain didn't swear. With a last, wide-eyed, look of despair, Wilkins turned and ran out through the kitchen. The door shut slowly behind him.

For a brief moment, the Captain thought of his wife and kids, about how simple it would have been to walk out the door and leave Wilkins to his fate. He felt shame at even thinking it, and the shame flared into rage. He wasn't going to make it easy for his enemies. He lowered his body, bending at the knees. He set his stance, ready to fight.

But where were the Unit staff?

*   *   *

8:00am

WILKINS STOPPED THE VAN IN the circular drive in front of Unit Eight, parking far enough off to the side to allow other patrol vehicles room to pass. He reached into his pocket and took out a bottle of eye drops. "Damn contacts keep drying up," he stated when he saw the Captain watching him. "Dave," the Captain said, "You don't wear glasses." "Well, if I did, that'd be why my eyes hurt!" Letting it pass, the Captain opened his door. He ducked his head getting out, avoiding losing a piece of his scalp to the door frame. Wilkins followed him into the unit and through the nearly empty dining hall and into the office, where they assumed their usual places, the Captain at the countertop that ran the length of the booth, Wilkins in the spare chair. Sergeant Warniski, the unit's regular, nodded at them and out of respect, took his long legs from the desk and stood. He brushed the mop of hair out of his eyes and without a word, he handed over sections of the daily newspaper that he'd "hidden" in his coat from Edna at the gate house. The aroma of fresh coffee permeated the office as the automatic drip maker gurgled to the end of a brew cycle. Did Warinski have some sixth sense that told him to put on fresh coffee for their arrival, the Captain wondered, or did he brew all day for the cheerful sound, pouring out what he couldn't drink? "Let me get you each a cup of mud," he said and returned with two ceramic mugs. "Dave," he said to Wilkins, "it looks like you need yours straight-up black. Cap, I got some cream and sugar for you." He set the coffee down like a Butler at an estate, then settled back behind his deck, again plopped his feet on the counter, and continued reading the paper where he had left off, no doubt working on a puzzle.

Wilkins read the sports section — his only interest — while the Captain took local and national news: stupid middle-east wars had claimed more American lives. The Captain wished the whole charade would end, and wondered if he'd been wrong to support the wars at the start. They had gone on long enough, at any rate, wasting lives, including that of a gung-ho boy whose mother Maura knew through her art and volunteer circles. That was close enough to bring it home for the Captain. He skipped to a story about a problem bear tranquilized in an apple tree. The mid-air photograph of the bear falling, relaxed as a rag doll, spread-eagle, made him smile.

Warinski was working the crossword puzzle and the "Word Search." He never chatted till he'd finished, though he'd glance down the hallways, from time to time, or into the dayroom to watch his inmate workers. It was the quiet time of day. The inmates who weren't at work or school had gone back to bed after count. The only ones moving about were swampers cleaning the dayroom and dining area. It was forty minutes before the next class would start, and most inmates slept to the last moment before leaving for the school complex. Until then, things were likely to stay quiet.

Warinski got up, poured them fresh coffee, and returned to his Word Search. The Captain flipped to the obituaries, and a name slapped him like a wet towel. "Hey guys, did you see that Pinky died?"

50

"No shit?" Wilkins put down his precious puzzle. "Man, what happened?"

"He only retired a few months ago," Warinski said, pressing the sports section to his chest.

When the Captain first came to work at North Woods, Pinky had been laboring for the state eight years longer than the Captain had been alive. Pinky — Sergeant Carroll Ellsworth III — was the highest seniority employee in the institution. His nickname came from the color of his skin; he was close to albino, with vivid red hair and blue eyes. He wore thick, plastic-framed glasses which often slipped down his nose as he talked. He was small, only about five foot six, with a pot belly over which he perpetually pulled up his pants and a shirttail that refused to stay tucked in, but because of his personality, he towered over his unit — and all of North Woods — a shirt, pudgy, friendly giant.

The Captain was lucky enough to be assigned to him for training. "Kid, my name's Pinky," the sergeant had said that first day, handing him his radio and keys. "Everything you need to run the unit is in these 2 books." Pinky plunked two slim volumes on the counter, the North Woods Rule Book and the Inmate Handbook. "Read 'em and get to know 'em better than the inmates do — and let me add just a couple things. *Never* trust an inmate; specifically, *never* let an inmate handle your keys — and *never, never, ever* do anything that's gonna get you or anyone else hurt." Pinky slid his chair from behind the desk and motioned the rookie forward to look at a list of inmates being punished. It had about a dozen names and looked like it was written in a foreign language:

Lopez, #36510, cell 21, 5-LOCA
Smith, #21779, cell 14, 30- LOE
Bingham, #71911, cell 02, 20-LOR
Quinones, #22639, cell 37, 15-LOP.
Linjer, #89876, cell 05, 5 24hr. rm. conf . . . .

"Sergeant Pinky, what are LOCA, LOE and LOR?"

"My name's Pinky, not Sergeant Pinky, as I already told ya," he said, leaning over and stabbing a meaty finger at the list. "Those are the punishments. LOCA is loss of commons area — Lopez can't use the dayroom, rec' room, laundry or phones. LOE means loss of electronics — Smith loses his radio and TV for however long is listed. See? Thirty days. LOR means loss of rec. — Bingham can't go to the outside rec' or the gym. LOP is loss of phone privileges, and this here is twenty-four-hour room confinement, which means that Linjer can only leave his cell to eat, go to the bathroom, get a drink of water, go to the infirmary or go on a visit."

While the rookie worked, Pinky watched, and to this day, the Captain heard Pinky's voice over his shoulder as he made his rounds. "Kid," Pinky'd say, "get to know your inmates. Know which one is into drugs, which one is into strong-arming. Know who smokes what kind of cigarette, who's a thief, who's gay. Know who belongs to what gang. Know them as a group, but treat them as individuals. Let them see you as a person. Let them see you as someone they can trust: if you tell an inmate you're going to do something, you better damn well do it! Treat them the way you'd want to be treated if you were an inmate. If you want to be respected by them, you have to respect them. You may not like what they've done, or why they're here, but that doesn't matter. They may be different colors, or different religions, but that doesn't matter. What matters is that you treat all of them fairly. If you don't, they'll call you on it."

Pinky made it a point to see the world of North Woods through the eyes of an inmate, a perspective that sometimes made the Captain's skin crawl. "They're going to be watching you more than you watch them," Pinky would tell him. "They'll know when you make cell checks, what kind of soda you drink. If you smoke, they'll know how much and what kind, menthol or regular. Even if you don't tell 'em, they'll find out whether you're married and if you have children, where you live and your phone number. They have twenty-four-hours a day to watch us. They have twenty-four-hours a day to find our strengths and weaknesses. They have twenty-four-hours a day to figure out ways to beat the system."

When Pinky saw the rookie looking a little overawed, he bucked him up with another dose of reality. He hiked his pants up and continued. "Our advantage is that no matter how long they plan and scheme, they usually screw it up! These guys aren't in the joint because they're rocket scientists. They're in the joint because they're lazy and impulsive. They're in the joint because they screwed up and got caught! Most have never held a steady job. Very few graduated from high school. They're street-smart, but they don't have enough common sense to pour piss out of a boot, unless the instructions are written on the sole. A lot of inmates, especially those from the inner city, never traveled more than fifteen miles from home until they came to prison. Most have never seen, let alone touched, a white-tailed deer — or a cow, for that matter. The only fish they've ever seen came frozen in a package."

Pinky's monologues used to confuse the Captain, who had studied Criminal Justice intent on being a cop, before backing into prison work. Pinky's lectures came at him like a fire-hose of criminology, army tactics, school-teacher tips, and parental wisdom. "Don't sweat it, Kid," Pinky would say, "It just takes a little time. For the first couple of weeks, the inmates are going to test you. They're going to see how far they can push you and what they can get away with. If you have any doubt when they ask for something, tell them no. It's a lot easier to change a "no" into a "yes" than it is to change a "yes" into a "no". You'll catch on. And if you don't, they'll eat you alive!" Day after day, Pinky lectured the rookie as they worked, alternately reminding him that he'd never know enough and that it was okay.

After forty-five years, Pinky had finally retired. The Captain had seen him about two months ago, in his bright red Oldsmobile in the parking lot, waiting for his wife, Mary, the civilian records clerk. "Hey Kid," Pinky yelled, "If I had as much time left as you, I'd jump off a cliff!" Even after all of these years, Pinky still called him "Kid."

"Pinky, you old goat!" the Captain said, shaking the mottled pink hand. "I didn't think they'd let you out in public anymore!"

"I'll tell ya what, Kid, it's too bad ya gotta wait 'til you're old to retire! I'm lovin' every minute of it! Mary's gonna hang it up next month, and we're really gonna live!" He was grinning like a fox with a chicken in its mouth. "Our daughter just gave us a grand-daughter to spoil. We haven't seen her yet — they live out east — but in her pictures, she looks just like me!"

"So, she's pink and fat? Congratulations, Grandpa!" The Captain gave Pinky a thumbs-up and headed for the gatehouse. "Stay in touch," he called, walking backwards.

"I will, Kid, I will. You take care, and don't let 'em wear ya out!"

Now Pinky was dead of a brain hemorrhage. "I don't think he ever saw his grand-daughter," the Captain said, tears forming in the corner of his eyes. Each man, turned away from the other as the obituary lay on the counter. Stunned, clutching their coffee cups like rosaries, they sat as still as children in church, each gathering their emotions'. After a minute or two, when they had each composed themselves enough to hide their grief from each other, they started talking again.

"That sucks," Wilkins said. "You work hard all of your life, and then you get — what? — six months to play."

They were silent for another moment. "Yeah, but Pinky enjoyed his time," the Captain said finally. "He could have retired years ago, but this is where he felt he belonged. His friends were here; his wife was here, the work kept him going." He folded the paper. "I hope I can enjoy my life to the end."

Wilkins nodded thoughtfully. "The funeral is Monday," he said.

"When I get up-front, I'll see if we're providing an honor guard," the Captain said. He had been to many funerals as an honor guard, and now Warinksi and Wilkins were both members. At funeral homes and gravesides, the guard — eight volunteer North Woods officers in full-dress uniform — did honors for their deceased colleagues: two at the doorway, standing at attention as people arrived; two at the coffin, one at the head and one at the foot; two with the family for support; and two standing by to give breaks. They acted as pallbearers when needed, stayed with the family at the graveside, and folded an American flag at the end, presenting it to the bereaved.

They would stand guard over Pinky, the Captain figured, knowing it was what he would have wanted. *Or was it?* The cantankerous old guy was full of surprises. Perhaps Mary would tell them if he'd ever mentioned such arrangements. It helped to know that the man in the coffin, as well as those he'd left behind, cared about it. The Captain cared. It meant a lot to him that there would be men like Warinski and Wilkins at his funeral, ready to show their respect for his family, life and profession. He hoped it wouldn't be for a while, but one never really knew.

Warinski sipped at his coffee, looking pensive. "Damn," he murmured.

"How's Emily, Tom?" the Captain said, shoving aside the gloom, seeking a grip on the present.

"Pretty good," Warinski said, smiling sheepishly. "You know, I'd thought she was ready to go away, but I guess I was wrong." He had sent his daughter, Emily, to college in Madison the previous year, and the leap from a sleepy Midwest town of three thousand to a city renowned as much for its party atmosphere as for its university had thrown her. Emily was a good kid; she just wasn't ready to resist the night life, and she'd failed as many classes as she'd passed — until Warinski and his wife brought her back to attend a local college. "It's going better," he said, pushing his hair out of his face. He shrugged. "Who knew?"

"So, I guess your only worry now is finding a Tutu big enough for your fourteen-year-old," Wilkins said, darting a sideways glance at Warinski and suppressing a smile. "It must be a real disappointment that the boy likes ballet more than hunting!"

"At least I have kids! The only thing you have is a bottle of Miller's and a cat!"

"At least my cat is a real boy!" Wilkins said. He threw a glance at the Captain; he liked banter all right, but he wasn't ready to mention his wife, Cindy's, pregnancy. The Captain marveled at Wilkins's shyness about his personal life. But in a way he understood. Warinski had enough self-confidence to be proud of his son's interest in dance, but the banter among North Woods officers tended toward narrow social norms. Who knew when your own quirks — or your families' — might become the butt of a joke?

The Captain's radio squawked to life: the transportation bus was due in about ten minutes. "I've got 'Captain' stuff to do," he said, taking a last gulp of coffee and standing. "Thanks for the coffee and entertainment." The crack of his knees as he unfolded his legs sounded like a stick being broken, causing Wilkins to remark, "Holy shit, old man! You gonna make it?" "Long enough to take care of your sorry butt." The Captain said as he walked to the front door.

Wilkins followed him out to the van, and they pulled up at the Captain's office as the orange-and-silver-painted DOC Transportation bus rolled to a stop at the front gate. There were no outside markings on the bus suggesting that it was from the Department of Corrections, only the "official" plates on the front and rear. If you looked closely at the darkened side windows, you could see bars on them, but it was impossible to see into the interior, where as many as fifty inmates sat.

They traveled shackled, hand and foot. One officer, armed with a shotgun and pepper spray, rode in the secured area, separated from the inmates by a heavy-gauge fence with gun slots; his compartment had a door and an emergency escape hatch to the roof. Three other officers rode up front with the driver, protected by a heavy steel security mesh that was never opened while the bus was moving and rarely opened at all outside the confines of a prison.

The officers radioed the final passenger count to the Captain, who gave the go-ahead to send the bus in and waited for it outside his office, holding his alphabetized transfer sheet. The inmates left the bus one by one, as the transportation officer called their names.

"Here's what's gonna happen," the Captain said. "I'll call each man's last name. When you hear yours, give me your first name, middle initial, institution number, and birthday. After I verify it, you'll take your property and follow the officer down to the property room for inventory. Then, as a group, you'll be escorted to Unit Sixteen, the barracks. You'll be programmed and evaluated for about two weeks, then sent to your permanent units." Some of the inmates looked sleepy after the ride, and he repeated the essentials, mindful of his old mentor Pinky's advice on their limitations. Usually, every third inmate would fail to give at least one piece of information. "Listen, people," he said, "I'll try to make this easy. But if there's anyone that doesn't know those three things, I can always give you time to remember them up in Seg'."

"Belmont," he said.   A muscular young black man stepped forward, scowling. By what contorted path, the Captain wondered, had a kid hardly older than LeAnn found his way into a gang and onward to prison? Belmont had tats up and down both arms: a crudely drawn machine gun the length of the right, and, surrounded by a flourish of barbed wire, a large "B-G-L" on the left — he was obviously a member of the Black Gangster Lords. His neck bore a name in cursive, "Q-Ball".

"Quincy R.," Belmont drawled, meeting the Captain's gaze. "097182. October twelfth, nineteen ninety-two." He kept "eye-balling" the Captain as he walked by and took a place in line.

'Why,' the Captain wondered, 'was Q-ball sizing him up?" "Calhoun," the Captain said, and an old-timer stepped forward.

"Henry L.," he said, in a voice as whispery as wind in dry grass, "01732, March fifth, nineteen forty." He looked almost grandfatherly, with salt-and-pepper hair and round glasses over soft brown eyes, yet somewhere in his past laid a long line of victims. With a number that low, Calhoun had started getting locked-up a long time ago.

"Black", the Captain said, looking up from his clipboard as a mid-sized, paunchy black kid stepped forward.

"Abdullah J., 575891, March fourth, nineteen ninety." Black, too, had "B-G-L" tattooed on his arm, and four teardrops on the left side of his face. He was a 'banger and a shooter: the teardrops symbolized either four victims or four shootings.

58

Another elder stepped off the bus next, a black man whom the Captain had known for years. "Chrystalman", the Captain called.

"William J., 30421, April 9th, 1942." Chrystalman kept his eyes on the ground, moving toward the captain with a stoop-shouldered shuffle. At about six-foot-six and skinny, dressed entirely in state greens, Chrystalman looked like a scarecrow, an old, broken convict. It was only when he looked up, with clear eyes and a genuine smile that his character showed. "Nice to see you, Bill," the Captain said quietly.

"Hiya, Cap" His voice was as deep and strong as ever.

"How's life treating you?"

"Going good, considering."

"Finally made it out of Max', I see. Still reading for the blind?"

"You bet. I get to read all the new best sellers, and it's nice to know that someone will enjoy listening to the recordings."

Chrystalman had been the first murderer the Captain had ever met — an inmate in the first housing unit he'd worked — and his story was tragic. A talented artist, he had, in his twenties, been well on his way to making a name in Chicago. But like many artists, he led a troubled life, and one night, high on heroin, he drove an hour north of the city and killed a Police Officer during the course of a drug store robbery.

Because his victim was a cop, Chrystalman knew he had no hope of ever getting paroled from a life sentence, and for thirty years, he made the best of it. The side-trip to Maximum Security was an unfortunate result of the arrival, a few years back, of a short, muscular mulatto named Clancy Lloyd.

Lloyd was, without a doubt, the biggest loudmouth braggadocio the Captain had ever encountered. "I'm probably the most intelligent, articulate man any of you will ever meet!" he'd announced, upon stepping off the bus, to everyone within earshot. "I'm a lover of women, a man of intellect! I've been all over and around the world, and there's nothing that I haven't seen or done! I know it will be a pleasure for you to get to know me. I hope the pleasure is mutual! Thank you!" With a flourish, Clancy had bowed and stepped into line.

The Captain was then a sergeant in charge of Unit Number One, and it was his bad luck, as well as Chrystalman's, that Lloyd was assigned there. "I'm Clancy Lloyd!" the stuck record had started again as the inmate arrived in his office. "I'm probably the smart' . . . ."

The Captain stood up, cutting him off. "Can the B.S.! I heard about your little speech, and you can spoon-feed the suckers your crap if they'll eat it. I'm not swallowing. If you ever make a speech like that in the dayroom and stir things up, I'll throw your butt in the hole so fast it'll make your head spin! I don't care who you think you are, or what you think you've done. In my unit you are no better and no worse than any other man." The Captain tossed him a cell key. "You're in cell thirty-two. Your room mate is Bill Chrystalman. Get your property stowed away and come on back. I'll let you know what I expect out of you."

The Captain hadn't wanted to put Lloyd in with Chrystalman, but the overcrowding gave him no choice, and much to the surprise of everyone, the two men got along, at least at first. Lloyd was able to tell Chyrstalman stories of places he could only dream of visiting, and Chrystalman had a soothing effect on Lloyd's amped up nerves.

Lloyd, as it turned out, was the youngest son of a wealthy businessman and had been around the world by the time he was eighteen. He was also hanging out with the wrong kind of people, by then, and getting into trouble. When Daddy cut him off, he took up crime — burglaries, mostly, and drug-dealing. He had been in and out of prisons across the country for twenty years by the time he wound up at North Woods.

Chrystalman and Lloyd became such good friends that Chrystalman's wife started letting Lloyd's girlfriend ride with her to visit. Twice a week, the women made the sixty-mile drive from Milwaukee to the prison. While the cell-mates got along fine, the women didn't. Chrystalman's wife was basically a hard-working, honest person, while Lloyd's girlfriend was a twenty-five-year-old schemer with four kids and no job. To make ends meet, she sold drugs - and herself. When she tried to recruit Chrystalman's wife to bring drugs into the joint, trouble flared.

Chrystalman's wife refused, and Lloyd started giving him a hard time. "I don't know why your bitch is bein' so difficult!" he told Chrystalman one morning in the bathroom. "All Chantelle did was ask her to bring a little dope."

"My wife isn't bringing any dope into the place," Chrystalman said. "She comes to see me, not to supply some fool's need."

Lloyd stopped brushing his teeth. "Man, you're some kind of old fool! You're gonna be sittin' here the rest of your life, and you done let the man break you! " The toothbrush wagged at the corner of his mouth. A fleck of toothpaste foamed on his lip. Chrystalman took a step back.

"You ain't even a man anymore!" Lloyd continued. "You're just an old washed-out convict sittin' in here doin' what you're told! You aint nothin' but an Uncle Tom! You shuffles yo' feet and 'Yah Suh, Massa, No Suh, Massa' and you nothin' but pitiful! That old lady of yours, she's just wastin' her time even comin' to see you! She could be out there livin' a good life with a good man, but she just wastes her life comin' to see an old broke-down fool!" He grabbed his crotch, leering. "Maybe when I gets out, I'll pay her a visit so she can 'member what a real man is like!", He bent over to spit out his toothpaste.

Chrystalman grabbed the back of his head and slammed his teeth into the edge of the stainless steel sink. "Listen here, you arrogant son-of-a-bitch! I've had enough of your smart mouth." He raised Lloyd's head about six inches and slammed it into the sink again. "The only time you had anything was when someone gave it to you. You're too damn stupid to realize that you blew the life God gave you!"

Chrystalman bent to look into Lloyd's bloody face. Water trickled from the faucet, and blood and teeth washed down the drain along with toothpaste and spit. "I blew mine too," Chrystalman whispered, "but I know that I can still do some good, even in here." Lloyd let out a low moan, and Chrystalman pulled him off the sink and threw him to the floor. The back of his head bounced with a hollow sound like a coconut, and his body quivered. "Tell that whore that you call a girlfriend that if she ever tries to call my wife again, I'll turn her in for selling dope. And if you ever talk to me that way again, I'll kill you! Remember, I have nothing to lose."

Chrystalman walked out, crossed the hall, and stuck his head into the Captain's office. "Clancy needs some help. I finally shut his mouth." he said. "I'll wait here for the white-shirt."

The Captain found Lloyd barely conscious, the sink and mirror speckled as though someone had flicked a wet brush of red paint. The pool of blood from Lloyd's head fanned out toward the drain in the middle of the room.

He lost eight teeth, as it turned out, and needed twelve stitches to sew up his head. His nose and jaw were broken; his mouth was wired shut for eight weeks. That meant he couldn't talk, a benefit as far as the Captain was concerned, and with his head shaved by the emergency room doc', he looked like a damn monk.

Chrystalman, of course, went to Max'. It troubled the Captain that Chrystalman was still in Max' when Lloyd got out of prison and moved to California. But six weeks after Lloyd's release, he bobbed to the surface in San Francisco Bay with thirty-seven bullet holes in his body and his tongue cut out. Evidently, someone else couldn't swallow his crap.

"How's the wife, Bill?" the Captain asked Chrystalman.

"She's doing fine. I've got a couple grandchildren and even a great-granddaughter. Stop by, and I'll show you their pictures."

"I sure hope they look like their Gramma," the Captain said, smiling. He reached out and touched the old man's shoulder. "Take it easy, old timer. I'll be down to see you soon."

The list was going well; every inmate remembered the drill. A light breeze had sprung up, and the Captain could smell the pines. It was shaping up to be a good day.

"Ingals," he called, looking up at another old-timer.

"James T., April 1st, 1963. Hey Cap, how'd you ever con your way into that job? The last time I saw you, you were a blueshirt runnin' a yard crew."

Ingals was a bit heavier, a little the worse for wear, but the Captain remembered him from a crew of ten years ago. "Well, Ingals, if you can't dazzle them with brilliance, you have to baffle them with bullshit! "

"You was always good with the B.S.," Ingals said with a chuckle.

The Captain laughed. Ingals had been twenty-three when the Captain first met him, with jet black hair and an easy disposition. At seventeen, he'd robbed a cab driver to supply a drug habit, but he was a good worker and a cheerful, calming presence on the crew. "What are you back in for? They make being ugly a crime?"

"Oh, I just got hooked-up in some stuff."

As Ingals joined the line, the Captain made a mental note to check his file and see what "stuff" he'd gotten "hooked-up" with.

The breeze was stiffening, a cloud had drifted over the sun, and Chrystalman, standing in line, looked cold, his long skinny arms around his chest. The Captain stepped it up.

"Nelson," he called, and recognized, with a start, a husky black man with a face disfigured by burn scars.

"Leon. January 3rd, 1979," the man said, his thin lips barely moving. His voice was thick, clotted, almost a hollered whisper. His face was lizard-like, his eyes fixed coldly on the Captain.

A chill ran up the Captain's back, and he tried to tell himself it was because of the cloud blocking the sun. He knew he was lying, though, and forced himself to hold still as he confronted a true evil from his past.

Leon Nelson was crazy as a loon and meaner than a snake. He' been in prison for the better part of twenty years and had the physique of a weightlifter. As an "enforcer" for a gang of street thugs, he'd been convicted of beating to death a fifteen-year-old high school kid who had wandered into his territory. He was suspected, but never convicted, of the beating deaths of at least five other people. His reputation earned him an instant leadership role in the prison gangs, and he took to shaving every portion of his body to make himself slick and hard to hold onto in fights. At six feet, he was big enough to intimidate everyone, officers and inmates alike. He hated the Captain.

Nelson had hated the Captain from the moment, years ago, when he had first arrived on Unit Number One. Within days, Nelson was in seg., having sucker-punched an officer.

The Captain — the sergeant — had been first to arrive on the scene, tackling Nelson and taking him to the ground, where they'd battled furiously until back-up arrived. After catching an elbow in the eye and taking a couple of punches off the back of his head, The Captain was able to get Nelson into handcuffs.

Soon afterwards, Nelson had shown an expertise in making weapons, from dinnerware shanks to spears made of rolled up newspapers. He was restricted, in seg. to getting a bag lunch for all three meals, which meant that he lived on bologna or peanut butter sandwiches, a piece of fruit, a carton of milk, a Styrofoam cup of coffee, and a cookie. The meals were delivered in a brown paper bag though a low trap in the door, while he kneeled at the back of the cell, facing the wall. The only other things allowed in the cell, besides bedding, were a Bible and two or three novels off of the library book cart that came once a week. The Captain peered in at Nelson every fifteen minutes, and every time, Nelson threatened to kill him. "Someday, Motherfucker, it's gonna be your turn. Someday I'll be watching you squirm. Someday, I'm gonna kill your ass."

An inmate janitor smuggled tobacco and matches to Nelson, who had collected bags, cups, and milk cartons from his meals, flattening them out and putting them between the mattress and the steal framed bed. One day, about three weeks in to Nelson's lock-up, the Captain looked in to see him standing behind a three-foot mound of trash, including pages torn from the Bible and library books. He held a book of matches out for the Captain to see, then climbed onto the pile, stooped, and struck a match. The Captain radioed Control for an extraction team.

"Come and get me, Motherfucker," Nelson taunted, grinning, as the trash-pile caught fire. "Come and get me! I'll kill you when you open the door! I told you I'd kill you! Come and get me, Motherfucker!" His pants and shirt were starting to burn as the fire alarm blasted, its screech filling the air.

An officer came running and helped the Captain empty two fire extinguishers under the bottom door frame. Between the smoke from the fire and the powder from the extinguishers, it was impossible to see into the cell, but Nelson was screaming. The Captain, realizing they couldn't wait for the team, unlocked the door and stepped into the cell as smoke and powder poured out. Nelson stood in the middle of the fire, his clothes burned half off his torso, revealing patches of pink tissue. His hands and arms smoldered. His face was raw, contorted with rage and pain. He jumped at the Captain, who threw him to the floor, and as the Captain fought the flames, he kicked and grabbed at his ankles. "I'll get you, someday. I'm gonna fuck you up. Someday, I'm gonna kill you."

When the extraction team finally arrived, they strapped Nelson to a gurney for the trip to the hospital, while the Captain went to the E.R. for smoke inhalation and a few cuts and bruises — nothing much. In the hospital, with second degree burns on his hands and face and third degree burns on his legs, Nelson kept ripping off his bandages. After a few weeks, the doc' sent him to a mental hospital, and the Captain never saw him again. Until now.

The Captain checked Nelson off the list, moved him along, and tried to ignore the scowl twisting the disfigured face — and the apprehension tightening his own gut. Nelson's expression told him quite clearly that the years had served only to fuel the hatred. As Nelson joined the line, Belmont — Q-ball — gave a slight nod toward the Captain. The hair on the back of the Captain's neck prickled.

But there was no time to brood over surly inmates. Once the count was confirmed and the bus cleared to leave, the Captain returned to his office to find Thorson waiting.

"In my office," the security director said.

Every time the Captain got called to Thorson's office, he felt like a kid going to the principal's office, and his shoulder muscles tensed with old, imprinted anxieties. At North Woods, it meant he had made a decision with which the higher-ups didn't concur. Either that, or else the union had a beef. Either way, Thorson's office was a place he preferred to avoid. The Captain could see that Thorson was worked up, strutting ahead of him like a bandy rooster, and as he opened the door to his office, his face was red as a circus balloon.

Captain Annette O'Malley sat in a chair in the far corner, jiggling her legs, a note pad balanced precariously on her knees, a half-empty coffee cup cooling next to her on Thorson's big oak desk. *Great,* the Captain thought. O'Malley was Thorson's administrator, his second-in-command. She was all of five-foot-two, which made her the only supervisor shorter than Thorson. She was rail thin with perpetually tobacco stained fingers and teeth. She wore her hair in a bouffant as hard as a helmet, and somehow felt it necessary to second the director's every emotion with a nod of her head. She was, essentially, Thorson's lap-dog, seconding everything he said or did, backing nobody but him. Thorson had hired her away from a minimum security prison where she had never been trusted to be a line supervisor. At fifty-nine-years-old, she still smoked three packs of cigarettes a day. Next to the desk, an ashtray was already overflowing with butts, though

the day was but a couple of hours old. To the Captain, this signaled that she and Thorson had undoubtedly been discussing
something at length. While smoking wasn't allowed in the building, it was another rule that Thorson chose to overlook when it
benefitted him. Though Thorson didn't smoke, he knew that he'd
insure the loyalty of O'Malley if he allowed her the luxury. Otherwise, she'd have had to suffer the indignities of other staff and
stand in a huddle outside and smoke. The Captain knew she
wouldn't smoke while he was in the office. She didn't want to be
seen breaking the rules.

"Come on in and have a seat." Thorson said. He walked
around behind his desk and sat down. The Captain pulled up a
chair in front of him. "Why did you put that inmate — let's see,"
— Thorson peered at a legal pad — "Belson — in full restraints
yesterday, Captain? If the inmate didn't resist, why did they strap
him down, and if he was giving them trouble, why didn't you go
in with more force?"

The Captain took a deep breath — he'd need to tip-toe
through Thorson's minefield — and reviewed the events, searching for the right words. He'd gotten a call from Seg' that Belson
had swallowed some meds, trying to kill himself. He'd gone in
with a team to restrain him, and when Belson kept threatening to
kill himself, he'd made the call to have him strapped to the bed.
Thorson, obviously, wanted to pick apart the decision.

"The inmate was compliant," he said, groping for bureau-
cratic accuracy. "I used only the amount of force that was necessary."

"So, why did you strap him down?" Thorson crossed his
arms and leaned back in his chair. O'Malley scribbled ferociously.

The Captain had been in this minefield before. Pretty soon,
they'd be spinning in circles like kids on the Tea-cups at Disney

World. All he could do was keep his answers short and direct and hope for the best.

"He'd made a suicidal gesture." The Captain felt his frustration rising and slowed down, enunciating each word. "He kept saying he was going to kill himself — do whatever was necessary to take his life."

Thorson shook a stubby finger at him. "But the nurse said the meds he took wouldn't have killed him." O'Malley clucked and shook her head.

The Captain took a few deep breaths — auto-genic breathing, it was called, a tactic he had taught as a defense instructor — but he could feel his boiling point coming and knew that he'd blow like the boiler on a steam engine if he let Thorson get to him. Carefully, knowing that Thorson would push him over the edge if he were given the chance, he replied in a calm, controlled voice, "He didn't know they wouldn't kill him."

"What could the inmate have done to harm himself or the staff?" Thorson continued in his quest.

The Captain bent back a finger with each item and calmly explained: "He could have hanged himself. He could have rammed his head into a wall. He could have torn his wrist open with his teeth. You know the dangers to staff, sir. He could have attacked them when they tried to stop him. He could have spit blood at them. So I had him strapped down. The on-call psychologist agreed." His calm had worked to push Thorson to the edge, instead.

"I don't care what the shrink said." Thorson yelled, pounding a fist on the desk. "Belson should not have been strapped down. If you wanted to strap him down, you should have waited until he really tried to hurt himself." Captain O'Malley looked like a bobble-head doll, so enthusiastic was her nodding as she scribbled. "From now on, you will not strap-down any inmate until they have really done something to hurt themselves." Thorson glared, his sparse mustache twitching on his upper lip like a semi-bald caterpillar on a hot side walk. "You will not do so just because you *think* they may hurt themselves."

Another deep breath and the Captain tried again, plucking words straight out of the *Policies and Procedures Manual*. "I felt that a danger existed, not only because of what he had done but because of what he was telling me. I didn't want to see him or any of my officers hurt. Our policies and procedures justify full restraints when an inmate presents a danger of death or great bodily harm to himself or others. I will not wait until an inmate is bleeding on the floor. I will not expose my officers to physical attack and bodily fluids. Sometimes policy has to be interpreted — with common sense."

The director rose from his chair. "Are you saying I have no common sense?" He screeched. He stretched himself to his full five-foot-four, puffed out his chest, and strode around the desk. O'Malley rose and followed, her pencil still poised at the pad. He stood in front of the Captain, looking down on him. "Captain," Thorson said, "you will not strap-down anybody in such a situation again. Do you understand?"

"No sir!" the Captain rose from his chair, towering, and looking down at the little man and his minion. "I will not put my staff in danger, nor will I endanger the safety of any inmate. What you're asking is ridiculous!"

O'Malley looked incredulous: the audacity — to question Thorson!

Thorson strode to the door, yanked it wide, and stepped aside. "You will not strap down an inmate," he said between clenched teeth, "until he has tried to hurt himself. That is all."

There was no more hope of breathing in calm and better judgment; the Captain was all hot bile as he brushed past Thorson. "What I'm saying, sir," he said, "is that sometimes I have to make a call from the heart instead of the book." He stopped in the hall and turned to face Thorson. "But I understand that some people are more worried about the next step on their career ladder than on getting it right."

Thorson's looked like a stewed tomato. "Get the fuck out of here! And you'd better watch your ass!" He slammed the door.

Shit, the Captain thought as he headed back to Wilkins and the van. Thorson had pushed his buttons the way only Thorson knew how. The Captain hated to be questioned by authority — any authority — he could admit that. Anger and sarcasm bubbled not far below the surface, and when the boss turned up the heat, it was all over. He was like a lot of inmates, that way. Maybe that's why he could empathize. But he had let his mouth get the best of him; he could have used some of that common sense he'd mentioned. Thorson was right: he'd better watch his ass.

CHAPTER IV

The Captain watched Wilkins run out the door, heard the door close with a clang behind him, and felt his senses heighten. He knew he was on his own, yet he knew better than to let the fear he felt deep inside of his being, take over. He felt a resolve in himself to fight back. He knew how to fight. He taught people to fight and protect themselves. Now, he was going to have to use what he taught. He reminded himself of what he told his officers: "If you're fighting fair, you aren't doing it right. ' He was used to having Wilkins cover his back; they had worked together so much that each seemed to know what the other was thinking — yet now that he needed Wilkins more than ever, Wilkins had done the smart thing, obeyed his command, and left him. Shit. He grabbed his shoulder mic' and transmitted, "Code Red, Unit 16. Code Red, Unit 16, Code Red." He sounded strangely calm, robotic almost, like an airport recording of a mayor welcoming visitors to his city instead of a hostage putting the institution into lock-down mode.

Code Red meant that all other radio communication would be cancelled, and inmates would be escorted back to their units. Non-security staff, including teachers and social workers, would report to assigned areas to assist with security, food preparation and a myriad of other jobs normally performed by inmates. The Control Center, knowing that the situation was out of control, would forbid any attempt, in the short-run, to come to the Captain's rescue. A wave of nausea swept from his gut to his chest, and he sucked in his muscles, tamping it down; in Code Red, he was alone — for the moment anyway.

The broadcast would go out State-wide, so that every prison would gather forces and prepare to help. Each one had a SWAT team, and within minutes, all teams within a ninety-mile radius would be on their way. The state patrol would seal off roads to North Woods; the county sheriff's department would mobilize an armed force around the perimeter. And on the grounds, they'd be taking slow, deliberate steps toward a rescue: examining a roster of everyone on duty to see who was missing, ordering off-duty supervisors and staff to report for emergency assignments, double-covering every post in the locked-down units so there were multiple staff in positions that were normally covered by a sole officer. Managing a media circus, naming spokespeople and places for reporters to gather. Department heads with missing staff would report to Lieutenant Gaines, who would double check their status before listing them as hostages.

The Captain normally commanded the North Woods sniper team, but now it would be up to his assistant in that role, Captain Schmidt — Smitty — he of the delicate stomach. Captain Jim Hafbeck would gear up North Woods' SWAT team and consult building plans for an assault. Murphy, Warinski and six or seven others would be relieved on-post to join Hafbeck.

The Captain lowered his body and stood to face the onrushing inmates — hyenas galloping to be first at the carcass. There was no way he could make it out of the unit, but he would go down fighting. He knew he had to fight dirty. He knew he may very well be fighting for his life. He saw the mob of inmates between him and the front door, twenty feet away. It swung open, as though it were mocking him for closing the door behind him. He lowered his body and sprinted toward the crowd, the door and freedom, knowing the only way out was to go through them. He elbowed the first inmate in the mouth, easily knocking him out of the way. The next caught a forearm to the jaw, with a crack that echoed through the room as his jaw broke. Freedom was a few feet away! Off to the left. He saw a larger crowd running at him. He met them and threw a fist to the throat of the next man he ran into; the man gagged and went down. He threw his shoulder into the next inmate, knocking him out of the way. A hand grabbed at his shoulder, but he ducked under it, throwing his elbow into the assailant's ribs. He felt the ribs crack, heard a cry of pain.

Using his shoulder and the force of his weight, he bowled over two more inmates and sprinted for the door. He had the keys in his hand; five more steps to go — maybe he would make it after all! — when a mop handle caught him in the side of the head.

Pain exploded through his entire body His glasses flew off, and a liquid warmth ran down his neck. His knees buckled. The front of his white shirt, he noticed as he fell to the floor, was turning red.

He caught a glimpse of Sgt. Golden as someone hit her across the face and ripped her shirt open. He saw it was Dunbar, the inmate she had hassled over the sugar earlier in the day. "You'll be getting' some sugar now, Cunt," Dunbar yelled as he and three other inmates dragged her sagging body to a storage room. Two inmates he remembered from the bus were trying to bend his arms up behind his back, and he fought them as hard as he could, knowing he would lose, feeling his strength drain with the blood from his head wound. He could see old man Chrystalmann sitting on his bunk holding a photo album to his chest, tears streaming down his cheeks as he watched the Captain being pummeled. Whether the tears were from seeing the Captain being beaten, or from the realization that this was where he was living his life, one couldn't tell, and if asked, he probably didn't know.

A sharp, burning pain: an inmate kicked him in the ribs — the man he had elbowed. It was Calhoun, the old con from the bus with the soft brown eyes and the low number indicating a long history of crimes. "How do you like it, Bitch!" Calhoun screamed. He was holding his side, and tears streamed down his cheeks as he backed up to kick the Captain again.

The Captain struggled to remain conscious. His vision was dimming, as if someone were pulling a shroud over his face. Fuzzily, someone was shouting out orders.

"Get his keys and radio! Put the cuffs on that piece of shit!"
Hands tore at his equipment. The room rotated slowly. He was losing
it, but though he could tell that he was hurt, bleeding, and scared, he
was still the Captain. He knew others still depended on him.

*   *   *

Outside of the unit, Wilkins heard the "Code Red" and grabbed
his radio to confirm it: "Code Red, Unit Sixteen. Code Red, Unit Six-
teen. Be advised sixteen is locked down and secure. At least three
known hostages." He jogged the few feet to his patrol van. He glanced
over his shoulder and could hear the yelling and screaming from inside
of the concrete block building behind him. He was relieved to be out-
side looking in, but felt guilty leaving the Captain behind, knowing the
Captain was right in ordering him out. Yet, that knowledge gave him
no comfort. The first thing he saw, climbing into the patrol van, was the
Captain's half-finished bottle of Diet Coke in the drink holder. He
dropped his shoulder mic' to his lap, swallowed a lump in his throat,
and brushed away the start of a tear. He started the car, wheeled it
around, sped past the housing units to the admin building, screeched to
a halt, and jumped out.

Lieutenant Gaines, at his desk, was calling in off-duty staff from
the security office when Wilkins entered the room. "You okay?" Gaines
said. "You hurt?"

"Let's just get going," Wilkins said. "Nobody touched me." He
avoided looking at the Captain's desk. "I'll get the gear set up. Tell any-
one else from the team that I'll be in the negotiations room down the
hall."

Fifteen minutes later, at the command desk in the negotiations
room, Wilkins unconsciously tucked in the tail of his shirt before sit-
ting, as though neatness might heighten his powers, as though sud-
denly, everything mattered. Around him banks of phones and recording
equipment waited, and a dry-erase board, covering one whole wall,

stared at him blankly, expectantly. The negotiations room, thankfully, was off-limits in an emergency to anyone not on the negotiations team, including Thorson and the warden.

Wilkins sat back, waiting for his team members to be relieved of their posts or report from home. As lead negotiator, he was going to have to pull a rabbit out of a hat. He sat back and let his mind wander, knowing that in a few minutes, his mind would be so wrapped up in what was going on, he'd have no time for thoughts of his own. He thought of how Cindy, his wife, was worried that her small, rounded belly was unattractive to him, while to him, it represented a new life they created together. He wished now that he had allowed the doctor to tell the baby's sex, giving him one-less mystery to deal with. He thought of his long dead sister, still nineteen in his mind, and of the sadness he felt, knowing his child would never know their Aunt. His head had started to throb, from either the stress of the day, or from the the booze of the night before, or a combination of both. Maybe the Captain was right, and he should lighten up on the booze. He then though of last seeing the Captain, his boss, his friend. He thought of the door closing, perhaps sealing them both to a fate neither had wanted. He wasn't going to let the door close behind him this time without a fight. He wasn't leaving his Captain alone.

*   *   *

8:50am

WHEN THE CAPTAIN WAS HAPPY, he walked slowly, his shoulder's relaxed. When he was unhappy, he speed-walked, arms swinging, shoulders squeezing up thickly around his neck. He was definitely speed-walking, breathing fast, and yes, his whole upper body was tense after the visit with Thorson. He stopped and took a few autogenic breaths, in through the nose, out through the mouth.

"What's up, Cap?" Wilkins said as the Captain climbed in. "Your butt looks smaller. Did Thorson chew off your ass for ya?"

"He took a little chunk, but there's plenty left for you to kiss," the Captain said with a thin-lipped smile. "Let's hit some more units."

The Captain made it a practice to visit each unit at least every other day; he and Lt. Gaines traded off, so that a white-shirt reached every unit every day. Most officers appreciated it, but some for some, it was a pain in the butt. They had to stash their reading, turn down their AM/FM radios, and bring the unit log book up to date.

The Captain could tell which sergeants were dealing well with the inmates. In those units, the inmates rarely approached him with questions. They knew they could go to the unit officer. In some, though, the Captain would hardly be through the door when a dozen inmates barraged him with questions, all of which could have been answered by the sergeant. Sometimes the Captain answered their questions; sometimes he deferred them to the sergeant.

In Unit seven he and Wilkins hadn't even made it to Sgt. Alex King's office when the Captain heard the familiar, "Hey Cap, you gots a minute?"

He stopped, and a lean, thirty-something Hispanic inmate approached. "I was wondering if I could ask a couple of questions?"

"Fire away," the Captain said.

"OK, you see, it's like this. I ordered thirty-two dollars worth of canteen last week, and they forgot half my shit. My Mama sent me in fifty dollars, so I know I had enough money. I didn't get no potato chips, Raman noodles, Snickers, or the two-boxes of Ho-Hos and three bags of pork rinds. A bunch of other shit too: I didn't get me any. . . ."

The Captain held up a hand. "Did you sign the receipt when they delivered your canteen?"

"Well, I suppose."

"Did you check the bag before you signed?"

"I was getting ready to head to the day room to watch TV, so's I was in a little hurry."

"That's not what I asked." The Captain cocked his head, looking intently into the inmates brown eyes. "Did you check your bag?"

"No, but I thought it was all there."

The Captain sighed. "The rules state that once you sign the receipt, you're saying that you have received everything you ordered. Did you save your receipt and order form?"

Grinning broadly, the inmate handed both the receipt and the order form to the Captain.

"Here's the problem," the Captain explained, "If you look at the order form and the receipt, it says that you only had enough money on your account to pay for part of the stuff. If you don't have enough money, canteen policy is to give you your hygiene products before they fill the other items. Did you get your soap, toothpaste, deodorant and stuff?"

"Yeah, I did, but that's bullshit! My Mama sent me the money! There should have been enough to get everything!"

"Before you get too worked up over it, think about this: the money probably came in too late to get into your account this week. It should be there next week. If it's not, let your sergeant know, and he can call the business office and run a search for it. I know that doesn't do you much good now, but that's about all I can suggest. OK?"

"I guess I'll just have to live off State shit until I can buy me some food." The inmate turned away, throwing over his shoulder the hint of a smile. "Thanks, Cap"

"There's a good example, Dave," the Captain told Wilkins. "Sgt. King probably gave the same answer I gave, but acted like he was doing him a favor. I keep telling you guys, we're here for the inmates; they aren't here for us. We're here by choice, they aren't. Our job is to address their questions, needs, and problems. We don't have to like them but we have to deal with them. If you treat them like dirt, if you don't show them at least a degree of respect, they won't respect you. They may fear you, but fear is a poor substitute for respect." When he thought about it, he was starting to sound like Pinky.

Some officers got the message, others followed Thorson's model. Staff and inmates alike feared Thorson, but behind his back, they laughed at him — or despised him. So be it. The Captain hoped that any fear an inmate had for him came from respect for the way he did his job, not because they detected an intent to intimidate or belittle.

Unit seven was an SMU, a special management unit or, as the officers called it, a smurf unit, after those little blue cartoon critters. The last housing unit the Captain had been assigned before his promotion was a smurf unit, and he had a soft spot for smurfs.

A smurf was an inmate with mental problems, and in the SMU, they were supposedly treated one-on-one for their problems. Unfortunately, the treatment amounted to one ten-minute session a month with a psychiatrist. In just ten minutes, the shrink would evaluate and medicate "as necessary;" the unit's thirty-six inmates were pretty much doped up on Thorazine or Valium all the time.

The Captain and Wilkins found Sgt. King looking out the window of his office at an inmate who was pacing the dayroom. King was a stout black man with short-cropped hair, graying stubble, and a high-school education from back in the Bronx. He was a smart guy with a big heart hidden behind a rough exterior, and — usually — a lot of patience

"Look at Cruiser," King said. Cruiser, who looked like a young, ugly, humorless version of Ernest Borgnine, was normally on so much Thorazine that all he did was shuffle back and forth down the hallway or sit in the reading room looking at comics in the newspaper, sucking on his tongue as if it were a huge, pink pickle; his medication dried out his mouth. But now he was talking to himself, gesturing with his beefy hands, alternately scowling and flashing gold teeth as he laughed.

"I've got the willies, and I can't shake it," King said. "He ain't normal. I mean, he ain't normal *abnormal*. That's why there's nobody else in the dayroom."

The Captain chuckled, shrugged, and laid a hand on King's shoulder. They watched a while.

"As long as he takes his med's, he's fine," King said, "but we can't force him. You know dat, Cap He says he don't need 'em. We notified clinical services; they said he's scheduled to see the doctor in a couple of days, and in the meantime we jus' watch him. But you know as well as I do how violent Cruiser gets when he doesn't take his med's." King shook his head, bit his lip. "It's been four days, Cap"

The Captain crossed his arms, watching. "Well, let's take a stroll," he said finally. "Let's take his pulse."

They took the long way around, exiting the office into the kitchen and strolling the cellblocks, getting a read on other inmate activity. The corridors were quiet; even the smurfs often had work or schooling of some kind, and those who didn't were holed up. Even in a drug haze, the smurf knew when something — or someone — was haywire.

"Hey, Kenny," the Captain said, nodding across the reading room at an inmate as big as a linebacker. Kenny had the mentality of an eight-year-old, and the only thing he wanted in life was to be an All-Star wrestler. When he wasn't watching wresting or looking at picture books, he was usually mopping.

Kenny looked up from the Big Book of Athletes and beamed as brightly as a searchlight. Kenny idolized the Baron, a professional wrestler who incorporated a move called the Claw. On any given day, it wasn't unusual for Kenny to creep up behind an unsuspecting smurf, yell in a high-pitched nasal voice, *"The Claw!"* and grab the inmate on top of the head like he was palming a basketball. The victim would let out a scream, and King would run to see what was happening, only to find Kenny doubled over in laughter, the victim cussing and rubbing the top of his head.

Only a week ago, the Captain had watched from the window of King's office, as Kenny, beaming, had crept up on Cruiser, who sat in the reading room, immersed in Charlie Brown — no doubt pondering the psychological implications of Lucy's underlying hostility toward men. The Captain and King had hustled out of the office in time to see Kenny clutch his right wrist in his left hand, raise it over Cruiser's head, and bring it down, screaming, *"The Claw!"* Cruiser's arms flew into the air, the newspaper following. With a high-pitched scream, he slid off his seat, knocking his cup of coffee off the table and landing on his knees, his eyes as big as Frisbees. As the coffee spread on the tile, a wet spot spread across the front of Cruiser's pants. The Captain's yelling finally got Kenny's attention, and he relaxed his grip. In any other unit, Kenny would have ended up in segregation. With the smurfs, you played it a little differently. Kenny and Cruiser cleaned up the mess, Cruiser got clean laundry, and life, as it was, continued. That's how easy things were with Cruiser when he was on Thorazine.

"It's a fine day, ain't it?" Kenny closed his book.

"Sure is," King said with a nod. He turned to the Captain. "He's the only one dares be out," he whispered. "I ain't kiddin'.

"So long, Kenny," the Captain said. "No more Claw for a while now, you here?"

"I got it, Mr. Captain," Kenny said. "I know what you're talkin' 'bout."

The Captain and King crossed the hall, their footsteps echoing on the shining linoleum. "Look Cap," King said as they came up behind Cruiser in the dayroom. "He's gettin' weird."

Cruiser was carrying on an animated conversation with himself, his voice rising to the verge of hysteria as he paced, then dropping to a whisper and ramping up again. They'd both seen it before. He'd get to arguing with himself, and when other inmates came near, he'd start yelling. Two months ago, the Captain had sent Cruiser to Seg' for half-choking another inmate after five days of a self-imposed Thorazine drought. The incident had lost Cruiser a job in the laundry, and the Captain and Cruiser had never exactly gotten along since then, at least not when Cruiser was off his meds. Cruiser didn't have the brains to remember what day of the week it was, but he remembered the wrong he perceived the Captain had done him.

"Hello Cruiser," King said from across the room. "The Captain and I came to pay our respects, see how you're doin'." Cruiser wouldn't look at the Captain, except to fling him a fleeting, scorn-filled glance. For all the Captain knew, Cruiser blamed him for keeping him in prison at all. Never mind that Cruiser had been a serial rapist, one who, by all accounts, had relished the pain he caused.

"What's he got in his hand?" King asked. "Look, there's something dangling when he turns."

There was a rustling behind them, and they turned to see Kenny moving a mop slowly along the hall floor. ""Mr. Sarg'," Kenny whispered. "Watch out for Cruiser. He was talking to his-self at breakfast, and it sounded like he was psychin' himself up to try somethin'."

Cruiser stopped pacing and watched them intently, his hands behind his back, a small, smug smile on his gaunt face.

"He's trying to hide it," King said. They approached, stopping halfway across the room, and Cruiser tensed, knitting his heavy brow.

"Cruiser," the Captain said, "What do you have behind your back?"

"Nothin'."

"Let me see your hands," the Captain said.

"I ain't got nothin'," Cruiser said, "Just go on your way."

"Cruiser, let me see your hands," the Captain said.

"You wanna see what I got, I'll show ya," Cruiser screamed, launching himself at them. He rose what looked like a U-shaped bag, and as he swung it, the Captain side-stepped. Before Cruiser could turn around, the Captain shoved him into the wall, taking the breath out of him. He fell to the floor, landing on his stomach. King mashed his face into the linoleum. The Captain twisted his left wrist behind him; his right hand was stuck under his body. Getting the cuffs on could be a problem.

"Just calm down," the Captain crooned, like a parent soothing a child. "Quit resisting. Give me your right hand. Calm down and don't make it any harder than it has to be." They lay on the floor, breathing hard, intertwined as close as lovers. The Captain could smell Cruiser's sour breath, hear him softly crying, feel his body quaking. Slowly, Cruiser's hand came out, and the cuffs went on.

King struggled up and extended a hand to the Captain. They helped Cruiser to his feet. On the floor lay his improvised mace: a long athletic sock holding, the Captain discovered a combination lock and a bar of soap.

Their body alarms had gone off, and within seconds, back-up officers would arrive to take Cruiser to Seg' and maybe, from there, to the Hospital for the Criminally Insane.

"Shit," the Captain thought, as he headed back to Wilkins and the van. "I probably should have left that problem to King."

CHAPTER V

Even in a semi-conscious state, the Captain could feel hands tearing at his equipment, hear the gold name tag being ripped from his shirt. Warm spit ran down his face. Someone jerked his arms in front of him, and handcuffs clicked over his wrists. A couple more punches glanced off the side of his head.

"That's enough now," someone shouted from far away. "Off him!"

As he drifted in and out of blackness, the Captain saw an image of Japanese troops in the aftermath of Pearl Harbor, a photo from some traveling exhibit. They looked invincible, unaware of the sleeping giant they'd awakened. It was a comforting image. He awakened to a voice rising above the others, apparently in command.

"That's enough! If he's dead, he ain't no good to us. Q-Ball, take him and put him in the office with the others. Don't let anyone hurt him. Everyone else, get stuff against the doors. We're in some deep shit now! A couple of you guys watch the windows, and let me know if you see anything. This ain't gonna be pretty."

The Captain feigned unconsciousness. He wanted to gather his senses before he opened his eyes, rather than risk being beaten unconsciousness before he could assess anything. He was vaguely aware of other hostages in the room; he heard someone else moan. He heard, in his mind, the kitchen door slamming shut as Wilkins left. He'd saved Dave, but at what cost?

*   *   *

"Let's head up to Seg'," the Captain told Wilkins after finishing the paperwork on Cruiser and the smurf unit. He made sure to duck his head as he climbed into the van. "I'm doing hearings today," he said, "I think about four or five." Wilkins, at the wheel, gave him sympathetic thumbs down. Thorson had sent the e-mail assigning the Captain the disciplinary hearing, which meant that it would be up to him to decide the guilt or innocence of inmates who had received conduct reports. He'd be judge and jury, really, determining the punishment of those he found guilty. In the past, the Captain had covered disciplinary complaints ranging from talking in the dayroom to assaulting a staff member, and meted out punishments ranging from verbal reprimand to a year in segregation.

"Why doesn't O'Malley do the hearings?" Wilkins said.

The Captain sighed. "Dave, she doesn't know her ass from her elbow. Do you think she can make a decision without Thorson telling her what decision to make?"

"You got a point there." Wilkins shook his head. The drive to seg. was a short one, and both men enjoyed the ride in quiet. Wilkins parked by the rear secure door, and the Captain scraped the top of his head getting out. Wilkins pretended not to have seen it, but the Captain, rubbing his head, caught him smiling. He reached back in the van and grabbed his bottle of Diet Coke, and he and Wilkins walked up the steps to the rear door of seg.. The Captain pressed the buzzer.

"Man, I don't know why you do that," Wilkins said, tugging at his wrinkled shirt-tail. "You know it plugs the Colonel in!"

The "Colonel" — Sergeant Theodore Dixon — could see all comers on a video monitor, and hated to have the Captain beat him to the buzzer. The Colonel was only a year older than the Captain, and they had started at the Academy on the same day, when both were newly married. But their home lives had taken different paths, the Colonel's to a bitter seven-year marriage and a contentious divorce. "Who pushed *my* button?" the Colonel growled, sounding for all of the world like the Wizard from behind the curtain.

"I did," quipped the Captain. "Is that a problem?"

The door buzzed, and the Captain and Wilkins entered a foyer with a second secure door. Before the Captain could press another buzzer, the Colonel opened the door, and they stepped into the outer rim of seg. Officers going about their daily business in various secure wings paused to wave through the glass. There were four officers besides the Colonel assigned to the seg unit. The Captain recognized Jones and Munson working in "A" block, and caught a glimpse of Officer Justin Katz in "B" block. Katz was a known brute, and the Captain didn't find him to be as trustworthy as Jones and Munson. Whereas Jones and Munson did their job, Katz, it seemed had the ability to stir up more crap than he should. In the bubble — a fourteen-by-eight-foot glassed-in control room — they could see the Colonel at his desk. With long sideburns, a handlebar mustache, and a goatee, the Colonel looked like a Confederate Officer; hence the nickname. The glass around him was called "ten-hour glass" because under testing, it took a minimum of ten hours of pounding with hammers to crack it. From his desk in the bubble, the Colonel controlled every door in the unit. Cameras pointed at all interior and exterior entrances beamed into his monitors. Separate TVs showed each of the four cell blocks, where the officers went about their business. Before the Captain could press the buzzer, the Colonel popped open the door of the bubble.

The Colonel through the Captain his usual scowl; the Captain knew it was all an act. The Colonel had loved his ex-wife, she had cheated on him, his heart had broken, and the frown was there to mask loneliness and pain. "You got a thing about pressing my buzzers, doncha?" the Colonel said.

"I guess I do, Ted." The Captain reached out a hand to shake. "How's seg' going today?"

"The usual." The Colonel tilted back in his chair, checking his computer screen as they talked. "Wilbert flooded his cell, so we turned the water off. We've been doing fifteen-minute checks on him. A couple of gang-bangers are yelling threats down the block to some gang-bangers that wear a different color. Gunther threw his food tray at Officer Beahm, so he gets bag lunches for the next week. A few are bitching because they don't like their celly." The Colonel glanced up, his mustache ends twitching downward with his frown. "The usual.

"Life's rough in the Colonel's mansion," the Captain laughed. "I'm here to dispense justice in a fair and equitable manner."

"You're dispensin' something, but I wouldn't call it justice! More'n likely you're gonna cause me extra work. How many we gonna keep?"

"I haven't looked at the tickets, but I suppose a couple will be here for a while. Let's get started." The Colonel buzzed the door open for him and the Captain met Wilkins and two segregations officers, Jones, a tall Al Bundy Look-alike and Munson, a stocky weight lifter that could, no doubt, lift the Captain over his head. Together they walked down the corridor to the hearing room, a small cube opening off a secured hallway. Wilkins held the door for them, then took a round tin of tobacco out of his pocket. He slapped it between his finger and thumb five or six times, then opened the tin and put a fresh clump of peppermint chew behind his lip.

"Now," he said, "I'm ready to work."

A table stood bolted to the floor in the middle of the room with a single computer monitor on top of it. A cushioned round seat was bolted to the floor in front of the table. There was room behind the stool for the two officers to flank a seated inmate. Opposite the inmate's stool, three chairs would accommodate the Captain and, if they ever chose to come, Thorson and O'Malley. A cabinet behind the chairs held documents relevant to the hearings: a clipboard that held the conduct reports for the Captain to read to each inmate was sitting on the table. Organizing the reports in front of him, the Captain took a cursory glance at each one and knew he was in for some bullshit excuses.

The Captain seated himself in the right-hand chair, and after making sure the proper forms were on the computer screen, he took a long pull from his Diet Coke, and set the bottle to the side. "Now," he announced, "I'm ready for some work," and nodded at Wilkins to take the seat to his left. "Bring Gibbons in," he said. Jones and Munson left to get the shackled inmate. The Captain glanced at a video camera jutting from the wall above the door. It used to have audio recording capacity, but a car thief had written a complaint on Thorson for calling him a "baby-raping, low-life, worthless piece of shit." The Warden had reviewed the tape and read Thorson the riot act. Thorson had made sure it would never happen again. With his own hands, he'd torn the audio wiring out of the video recorder. A small brown wire dangled from the neck of the camera. Evidently nobody had gotten around to repairing it.

The hearing room door swung open, and a scrawny, young white inmate with a throwback mullet that reached to his neck, mated with sparse sideburns, much like the Colonel's, stepped into the room wearing an orange jumpsuit, his hands cuffed behind his back. He had leg irons on as well, and the Captain couldn't help but smile as the inmate tried to adjust his walk to the long-legged stride of Jones, but came up short every step when he reached the end of the chains. Gibbons was a walking billboard; the Captain studied his copious tattoos as though they were Oneota cave paintings holding clues to ancient rituals.

Three tear drops descended from Gibbons's right eye, which meant he had either been the driver or the shooter in three drive-by shootings. On his right upper arm, an upside-down crown showed disrespect for a rival gang. On his left upper arm, a crude figure of a naked woman paid tribute to "Brandi:" No doubt it was true love. On Gibbons's right forearm, crude letters spelled his own nickname, ""G-Man," while on the knuckles of his right hand was L-O-V-E and on the left, H-A-T-E. Barely visible under the open "V" neck of Gibbons's jumpsuit was an ornate " 𝕃𝕒 𝔍𝔞𝔪𝔦𝔩𝔦𝔞," showing cross-cultural allegiance to a Mexican street gang.

It was the dubious artwork of a jailhouse entrepreneur working in dull blue ink. At least it appeared that everything was spelled right. The Captain had seen plenty of jailhouse mis-spellings, forever marking the man not only as an ex-con, but as an imbecile as well!

"Inmate Gibbons, #130351, you are charged with violating three counts," the Captain said as the Seg' officers marched Gibbons to the stool. Gibbons slouched, looking at the floor.

The Captain read rapidly, enunciating carefully, so that the words came out with a rat-a-tat urgency. "They are 33.28, Disruptive Conduct, 33.24, Disobeying Orders, and 33.27, Fighting." He looked up. Gibbons stared at the floor. "The report reads: At 12:25pm on 9-19, I saw inmate Peter Gibbons argue with inmate Harold Ziegler. Inmate Gibbons yelled at inmate Ziegler, and pushed him. I then saw inmate Gibbons strike inmate Ziegler in the face with a closed fist. Inmate Ziegler struck inmate Gibbons back, also in the face, causing inmate Gibbons to fall to the floor. Inmate Ziegler then turned to walk away, and inmate Gibbons called him a 'punk-ass Fag.'"

The report was by Sergeant Warinski, who could write better than most officers. His precise and grammatical reports made the necessarily dry prose almost comical at times. "I ordered the inmates to go to their cells, and inmate Ziegler did as he was told. Inmate Gibbons continued to yell at inmate Ziegler, creating further disruption in the unit. Lieutenant Gaines and a patrol came to the unit and removed both men to segregation. End of report." The Captain looked up. Gibbons sat erect, his arms crossed. "Are you guilty or innocent of the charges?"

"Man, this is bullshit," Gibbons said, licking his lips nervously.

"That's not what I asked. Are you guilty or innocent?"

"Man, dude got all up in my grill! He started talkin' shit about how him and his homies is runnin' stuff and I tol' him that all they's runnin' is they moufs! He tol' me he'd kick my ass, an' I said, 'bring it, punk,' and dude pushed me! Motherfucker had no right puttin' his hands on me, so I blazed him."

The Captain leaned on the counter, hands clasped, eyebrows raised. "So, what you're saying is that you got into an argument, he pushed you, and you hit him. Is that correct?"

Gibbons put his hands on the table and leaned forward, his face close to the Captain's. "Damn straight! Ain't no bitch like that gonna put hands on me!"

"So, what happened after you hit him?"

"The bitch sucker-punched me! Then the sarg' came along and told us to go to our cells. He's lucky the sarg' stepped in or I'd 'a fucked him up!"

The Captain leaned a little closer, his eyes locked on Gibbons's blue eyes. "After the sarg' stepped in, did you go to your cell as ordered?"

"The bitch did. I was a little worked up. I still wanted a piece of him."

"OK," the Captain said, "is there anything else you'd like to add?"

"Nah, just the bitch had it comin'."

All of the while Gibbons was talking, the Captain was typing his remarks on the computer, trying to keep up. He wished that he had a stenographer. When he was finished, he read each statement back to the inmate to make sure he got it right. "Is that accurate?" he asked. "Yeah, that's what I said." The cocky little con replied. "OK." The Captain said, motioning the two officers to take Gibbons out of the room while his fate was decided.

Jones and Munson stepped close and took Gibbons arms, almost lifting him out of the chair before he could stand. He was taken to a holding cell down the hall from the hearing room. The administrative rules said that the Captain, acting as a one-man committee, had to make his decision in private. Wilkins, knew this, so with being asked or told, left the room to get a cup of coffee.

The Captain reviewed his record. Gibbons had been written up for fighting and disruptions eight times in the past year. Each time, he'd received a progressively harsher punishment — the last time: sixty days in Seg'. *Enough is enough*, the Captain thought, and typed his finding in the computerized form: "I conclude guilt based on . . . . " When he was finished, he radioed Jones and Munson to bring Gibbons back in. Behind them, Wilkins walked, holding a hot cup of coffee.

The Captain took a sip of his coke as Gibbons was sat on the stool. "Mr. Gibbons," the Captain said to Gibbons, slouched on his stool, "I'm finding you guilty of all charges. By your statements and actions, you disobeyed staff orders, engaged in a fight, and created a disruption in your unit. Your actions compromised security and created a danger of physical harm to another. This is your ninth write-up this year for the same thing. I'm giving you three hundred sixty days segregation. Under state law, you will lose one day of good time for each day of segregation. You will be transferred to a Maximum Security institution at the conclusion of your Seg' time here. Do you have any questions?"

Gibbons reared back as though he'd been slapped. He was a tough kid, but he was a kid, and this was more than he'd bargained for; he hadn't yet done hard time at Max'. Given his size and age, Gibbons would have a difficult time of it. At Max', he'd have three choices: depend on his gang to keep him safe; become a "punk" for a strong, influential inmate; or — with a lot of will and even more luck — get his act together and keep to himself.

The Captain doubted he was smart enough for the latter and as a white boy in a Spanish gang, his protection and influence was limited. That left becoming a "punk," a multi-faceted career choice. As a punk, it would be up to Gibbons not only to meet the sexual needs of a bigger, stronger inmate, but to clean his cell, do his laundry, help supply his canteen needs, and be willing to be "loaned out" to other inmates. A typical punk was loaned out often, for a few minutes or however long it took the borrower to achieve gratification by whatever means he chose.

The relationship between a punk and his protector was never long-lived. When staff caught wind of it, they were duty-bound to intervene — which usually meant placing both parties in segregation, where the punk would confess to the relationship, thereby sealing his fate not only as a punk but as a snitch. Then, both would be transferred to other prisons, where the cycle would repeat. It made the Captain sad, watching Gibbons blanch.

"Aint no thang," the little man said, "Aint no thang." Jones and Munson led him out, this time to the strip cell so he could be strip searched before beginning his sentence.

Next on the agenda was Oscar Banks, a regular at disciplinary hearings. Banks was a black man in his early twenties and a giant — six-foot, six-inches one-hundred and fifty pounds, a skin and bones giant. He had spent a lot of time hitting a crack pipe on the streets, and any brain cells he had left were dying of loneliness. On top of his addictions, he was classified as a smurf.

"OK, Mr. Banks, let's see what you did this time." He picked up a sheaf of papers.

"I aint done nothin', they's just messing wi' me!" Banks said, hunching dejectedly on the stool.

"Well, let's do this officially. The report says you are charged with violating rules 33.24, Orders, and 33.28, Disruptive Conduct."

"Awwww, booshit" Banks said, shaking his head, starting to stand as the officers on each side moved in . . . .

"Now just wait a sec'." The Captain patted the table. "Let's get through this. Just sit down before the officer is forced to make you sit."

Banks looked up at Officer Jones, decided that he wasn't going anywhere, and slumped back onto his seat.

The report reads: "On the stated date, I, Sergeant Golden saw inmate #174015, Oscar Banks, masturbating with his hand in his cell. Inmate Banks was naked on his bed with the lights on, and when I walked by his window, he looked at me. He didn't stop what he was doing, and continued to lie naked on his bed.

I have seen inmate Banks masturbating on several occasions and have warned him about doing it while I am working. He blatantly ignored my warnings. End of Report."

The Captain sighed and looked up at the giant of a youth huddled on the stool. "So, what do you have to say?"

"Captain, I din't even know the lady was workin'! I was on cell confinement and couldn't leave my house so I never even saw her! The oniest reason the light was on is my celly was readin'. If'n I'da know' Sergeant Golden was workin', I wounta' done nothin'. That lady don' like mens, and she shore don' do nothin' for me! Why, if'n I was thinkin' about her, I wounta been *able* to do nothin'! An' I swear, I never seed her in the hallway! That lady just don' like mens!"

The Captain laid the report on the table. "Banks, you know if Sergeant Golden is working, you've got to walk the line. Now, I don't believe you didn't know she was working. You say your roommate was reading. You mean to tell me he doesn't care that you're lying butt-naked on the bunk under his bunk playing with yourself? He thinks that's OK?"

Banks looked at the ceiling a moment, as though pondering a large question. ""Well, ya see, it's like dis: I tries to be real quiet. I don' move much, and most a the time, he don' even know I'm a doin' it!"

The Captain smothered a smile. "It says in the report you were masturbating with your hand. Is that what you usually do, or is it something new?"

"No Cap, it ain't somethin' new! I always be usin' my hand! Maybe she just ain't never paid attention befoe!"

The Captain frowned exaggeratedly at Banks, battling the smile muscles. "Oscar," he said, "why is it that I'm always seeing you on this petty stuff? Hardly a week goes by when an officer doesn't call and tell me that he's writing you up. You've been here long enough to know who's who, and you know what you need to do! I'm really tired of the whole thing! Maybe I should keep you up here for the next year or so. Do you think that would do any good?"

"I dunno, Cap, but I'll tell ya, if'n that lady's workin' my unit, I ain't never gonna touch my privates where she can see me agin! It just ain't werf all the trouble! Now, I guess I'm a guilty a the orders, 'cause Miss Golden did tell me befoe not to be a playin' with myself when she be on-duty, but I wasn't disruptive! Like I tolds ya, I tries to be real quiet, so's I don' bother my celly."

This was going to be a quick decision, and in defiance of the policies, the Captain pronounced his sentence without deliberation. "Inmate Banks," he said," I'm finding you guilty of violating 33.24 orders. There is no indication in the body of the report that your conduct disrupted the unit, and you said you were doin' it real quiet, so I'm dropping the charge of disruptive conduct. As a punishment, I'm going to give you thirty days' unit confinement. That means you can only leave your unit to go on sick-call, go to school, or go on visits. Do you understand?"

"Yessir, Cap, I understands. And don' you worry, I don' be touchin' mysef no moe when Miss Golden be workin'!

The seg officers took Banks out, and as the Captain waited for the next miscreant, his radio blared. "Code-One, Seg' Unit, Code-One, Seg' Unit!"

The Captain and Wilkins ran out of the hearing room and up the corridor to the control booth. Down one of the wings, the Colonel stood outside a strip-cell from which arose a dull thud, followed by a moan.

"Captain!" The Colonel turned, stroking a mustache tip nervously. "It's Gibbons. As soon as the officers put him in the cell, he started banging his head on the wall. He won't listen to me, and he's bleeding from a cut over his eye."

The Captain looked in through the slit of a window. Gibbons sat on the floor, a small cut bleeding profusely above his right eye. The blood streamed down his cheeks over the tattooed tears.

"Gibbons," the Captain said. "Are you OK?"

"Fuck you!" Gibbons screamed.

"Gibbons, I need to talk to you."

"About what, man? Just get the fuck away from me!" Gibbons staggered to his feet and launched himself head-first at the concrete wall.

"Gibbons! Stop!" the Captain yelled, as the inmate hit the wall and slumped to the floor. The Captain could have sworn he felt the "splat" reverberate up through his feet.

Lieutenant Gaines came running up the hallway, hitching up his pants under his sagging belly. "Suit up an extraction team," the Captain said. "I'll keep talking to him."

"Back in a jiff'," Gaines said, and disappeared down the hall behind the Captain. It was Gaines's responsibility, as second-in-command, to prepare and lead the First-Shift extraction — or entry — team: four officers trained to go into cells and restrain inmates who were suicidal or threatening.

"Mr. Gibbons," the Captain said, "what you're doing isn't hurting anyone but yourself."

"Like you give a shit if I kill myself, " Gibbons screamed. He was sitting on the floor, swaying blearily. "Like you or anyone gives a shit what happens to me!"

"Mr. Gibbons, if I didn't care, I wouldn't be here talking to you." The words flowed as they always did, but the Captain found himself thinking, "I care, right here and now, but the system can't protect this man, and I am part of the system, so in a way, he is right." "I want you to come over to the door so we can look at your forehead and move you to a single cell," he said, and he told himself, "Cut the double-thinking crap or you'll be useless to your family and fellow officers. Just cut the crap."

"You're only here because you have to be!" Gibbons screamed. "It's your job! You don't care about me or any other con! I'm nothing but a piece of shit, to you! Don't try to tell me you care!" As he talked, Gibbons got to his feet. He looked the Captain squarely in the eye and ran head-first for the wall, hitting it with another dull "splat" and falling to the floor. "There. How do you like that?" he said, bleeding from a fresh cut over the left eye. "Want some more?"

The Captain took a deep breath. "Like I said, you're only hurting yourself. What do you hope to accomplish by this? It's not going to change the past. You're only messing with your future. Now, I'm ordering you to come to the door, put your hands through the trap, and let us move you to another cell."

Gibbons was trying to get to his feet when Lieutenant Gaines arrived with his entry team, an officer with a video camera trotting up after them. It had taken Gaines less than five minutes to pull the officers from their posts. They'd grabbed their emergency bags, pulled on black jump suits, mouth guards, stab vests, gas masks, groin cups, elbow and knee pads, and black helmets with reflective face shields. They looked like Darth Vader in a repeating mirror.

"Inmate Gibbons," the Captain said, "if you refuse to come to the cell door, I've authorized the lieutenant to use force to make you comply with my legal, lawful order." He paused; no answer. "Do you understand? "

Gibbons approached the cell door window and looked through the slot at the entry team. Lieutenant Gaines held a collapsible silver baton in one hand, a Taser stun gun in the other. "Bring it, you Fags!" Gibbons shouted. "You think you're so tough in your goon suits! I'll kick all you all's ass!" He backed away from the window.

"Lieutenant Gaines, you are authorized to enter the cell," the Captain said.

Gaines took the Captain's place at the window. "Inmate Gibbons, I'm giving you one more chance to comply. Come to the door and be handcuffed. If you refuse to follow my order, I will have the team enter. If you resist the team, I *will* deliver a shock of fifty thousand volts to you until you stop resisting. Do you understand?" Gaines held up the Taser and activated the trigger with a loud crackle. The electricity arced like a bolt of blue lightning between the contact points. Usually, when inmates saw what they were up against and realized that there was no way to win, they gave up. Activating the stun gun often accomplished that.

"So, is that supposed to scare me?" Gibbons yelled. "You'll need more than that, you pussies!"

"Prepare to enter," Gaines said, and the team lined up, the lead man, Jones, with his pad in front of his chest, Munson and the rest tight behind him in a formation they called butts to nuts. "Inmate Gibbons, are you going to comply with my orders and come to the door?"

"Fuck you!" Gibbons screamed.

"Open strip cell!" Gaines radioed the control bubble. As the door crept open, the team pushed. Gibbons tried to squeeze out of the crack, but as it grew larger, the force of the combined weight of the entry team, about a thousand pounds, pressed him back. As the door swung wide, the team drove him into the back wall of the cell as easily as a freight train knocking a Toyota off the tracks.

Each member of the team had responsibility for a specific move or body part. Jones and Munson used their thick pads to trap Gibbons against the wall, a third Officer, Wilkins leapt over their shoulders and grabbed Gibbons around the head, pulling Gibbons with him as he dropped to his knees. Dropped their pads, Jones and Munson each grabbed an arm. By the time Gibbons hit the floor, his arms were pinned behind him. A loud grunt escaped him as they landed on him, but he still had the wind to struggle.

Lieutenant Gaines reached between the Jones and Munson and hit Gibbons with the Taser. "Quit resisting!" he yelled.

Gibbons's scream lasted the whole eight seconds of the shock. He went limp. The weight of the officers and fifty thousand volts of the stun-gun had finally done it. Violent, yes, but over in seconds, leaving Gibbons uninjured.

Wilkins let Gibbons's head let go and lay across his legs, while a fourth Darth Vader, Officer Katz latched leg irons on him and moved to secure his hands behind his back.

"Sir, stop resisting!" Gaines kept saying. "Calm down, don't resist!"

Two officers raised Gibbons to his feet, and he stood dazed and panting, the sad, naked curves of the blue-inked "Brandi" glistening on his wiry arm. The lead men slipped their arms through Gibbons's cuffed arms and walked him backwards out of the cell. The third man put a hand under Gibbons's chin and held his head back, covering Gibbons's eyes with his other hand. Gaines guided the ungainly procession to an observation cell.

"Mr. Gibbons, you are being placed on observation status because of your attempts to hurt yourself," the Captain said. "Strap him down."

The team cut the orange jumpsuit off Gaines and laid him, naked, on a thin mattress. They tethered his hands and feet to the bed frame, put padding under his head, secured his head and arms with a thick leather strap, and withdrew, leaving only the Captain and Gaines.

Gibbons lay on the mattress weeping. Glancing over, the Captain watched as Officer Katz leaned close to the inmate and saw, rather than heard him say something to Gibbons. The inmate started screaming and the Captain stepped forward. "Katz," he said quietly, "I don't know what kind of crap you're stirring up, and you're lucky I didn't hear what you said. Get your ass out of this cell." The Captain looked at Lt. Gaines and told him, "Katz is no longer to be used on the entry teams. Got me?" Gaines nodded in understanding. "Katz, drop your gear in the supply room. See your Sergeant and get back to work."

Now, it was back to the problem at hand. "Peter," the Captain said quietly. "Dr. Wilson is coming up to talk to you. I've got the nurse here, and she's going to clean up your cuts. You need to calm down. As soon as the doctor says its okay, we'll take the straps off, but you have to calm down." As he talked, the Captain checked the straps, making sure they weren't too tight. Gibbons slowly quieted down. "Are you hurt anywhere else?"

"I don't think so," Gibbons sobbed, "please let me up."

"Peter, I can't do that just yet. The doctor will have to talk to you first. We have to be sure you won't try to hurt yourself."

"I won't, I won't," Gibbons pleaded, "just let me out. I promise I'll be good!"

"Peter, the doctor is here. As soon as he says it's OK, we'll let you out."

"LET ME UP, YOU ROTTEN MOTHER FUCKER!" Gibbons screamed. "I'll kill you if I ever see you on the streets! I'll kill you! LET ME UP!"

"It's all right, Peter, you need to calm down," the Captain said, as matter-of-fact as though Gibbons had cut a finger or scraped a knee.

A nurse cleaned and bandaged Gibbons's forehead, and when Dr. Wilson bent to talk to him, the Captain and Gaines moved to the back of the cell out of his line of sight. Dr.Marlin Wilson was a tall skinny white man with straight black hair; a deep, soft voice, and a loose-jointed way of moving that reminded The Captain of the Scarecrow in the *Wizard of Oz*. He leaned over the bed and talked with Gibbons for five or six minutes. "Peter, you're going to stay strapped for a while," he said, straightening. "I think you're a danger to yourself, and no one wants to see you hurt yourself anymore."

"FUCK YOU, AND FUCK THAT FAT-ASSED CAPTAIN TOO!" Gibbons screamed as the door closed on him. "I HATE ALL YOU COCK-SUCKERS!

"Well, Captain, Mr. Gibbons sure hates you, doesn't he?" Dr. Wilson said, leaning against the wall outside the cell and crossing his arms. "Right now, you're the reason he's in seg., the reason he's going to Max', and the reason he's strapped down. I think you're definitely off his Christmas list."

"Well, I'm sure that I'm on some list." The Captain had weathered so many inmate threats to kill him that they were starting to run together. He rarely thought about them.

What he thought about, as he returned to the hearing room after debriefing the entry team, was that Gibbons was only three years older than LeAnn. It made him feel sheepish for worrying about LeAnn. It made him wonder what had happened to Gibbons when he was LeAnn's age, or Marie's age, or a toddler, for that fucking matter. *Shit,* it didn't pay to think about that social work stuff. It wasn't his job, and yet the older he got, the harder it was *not* to think about it.

The rest of the hearings were the usual fare: disobeying orders, being disruptive, nothing as serious as Gibbons's infraction. He gave a couple of inmates Seg' time, the rest of them unit confinement, and he shoved down comparisons to his daughters or anyone else he knew outside of North Woods. It simply didn't pay to brood that way.

"Where to, Cap?" Wilkins said, as the Colonel, one step ahead, buzzed them out the doors.

The Captain heaved a sigh. "You're driving, you decide." It was clouding up. Maybe it would rain. That would be okay, he thought, ducking low to avoid bumping his head and closing his eyes as he settled into the vinyl seat. He could relax when he got home. Soon, he thought as he glanced at the clock on the dashboard. He reached for his bottle of coke. Taking a drink and emptying the bottle, he sighed again and thought of the days ahead, his days off. He had to work one late shift as a cop, tomorrow night, but the days were his. If it rained, he could even let the leaves go for another day. "What's one more day?"he thought. "There's always tomorrow."

CHAPTER VI

The Captain slowly opened his eyes and he saw Q-Ball. He remembered him — Quincy Belmont — from the bus that morning, when he'd had on prison orange. Now he was wearing gym shorts and state issued green t-shirt. His long legs were spindly, though his biceps were strong and defined, as was usual with prison weight lifters: the B-G-L of his Black Gangster Lords insignia stretched and bulged over the muscle. The Captain had never seen Q-ball before he'd stepped off the bus; he figured him no different from the other young, institution-raised gang-bangers. He'd probably spent his early years with a single-mother, grandmother or aunt, or he'd bounced from foster home to foster home, with a few stops at juvenile detention. Alone, he had probably been a relatively decent kid. With his gang buddies, he'd obviously become a mindless thug, determined to prove his manhood, regardless of the cost to others.

Q-Ball walked the Captain past the other inmates, motioning them back to be sure nobody got close enough to hit him. "You alls step back, this one's too valuable. We ain't gonna hurt him no moe, lessun they do somethin' stupid." A few of the inmates spit at the Captain, anyway. He prayed that nobody — on either side — would do anything more stupid than that.

Q-Ball led him to the unit social worker's office and shoved him in, following close behind, pushing him into an office chair. "You sit yo' ass down. Don't be tryin' to get up. I'll kill yo' ass if you get any ideas."

"Q-Ball," someone yelled, "don't you let no one hurt the Captain. Me and him go way back." The voice was thick, clotted, strained. It took the Captain a second to recognize it, and when he did, he knew his prospects had taken a turn for the worse. "If'n there's gonna be any hurtin' on him, I'm gonna do it my sef," Leon Nelson rasped. "I been waitin' too long to let anyone else do it. Me and the Captain have some catchin' up and a little pay-back to take care of"

*   *   *

11:15am

IN THE VAN, THE CAPTAIN and Wilkins tended to tease more as the morning wore on. Maybe it kept them awake. Maybe it reminded them of the outside world without quite taking their minds off North Woods. As they wheeled away from Seg', Wilkins asked the Captain when LeAnn would "be legal," and the Captain asked Wilkins if he'd enjoyed a six-pack before work to douse the headache with the "hair of the dog." Wilkins laughed, palpated his temple, and changed the subject.

"What do you think of the new mandatory sentences?" he said. Politicians had decided to get tough on crime, a couple years back, enacting mandatory sentencing. In the old days, an inmate would serve two-thirds of his sentence in prison and the rest under supervision. If he did what he was supposed to — kept out of trouble and made an effort to straighten up — there was always a chance for parole. Now, ten years meant ten years. Life meant life. It sounded good.

"The whole thing sucks," the Captain said.

Wilkins glanced over, his blue eyes wide. "When did you get soft? I thought you were a hard-ass."

"I didn't get soft. I just face reality. It sounds good to the public that if Joe Schmoe commits a crime and is sentenced to ten years, he'll do ten years. But what's he going to do in those ten years? Sit around watching cartoons, soap operas and CSI, and maybe go pump iron a couple of hours a day. He doesn't have any incentive to change. You've removed all hope of getting out early."

"At least he's gone," Wilkins said.

"That's true, but ninety percent of the inmates will be on the streets again, some day. Do you want some guy living next door who just spent fifteen years locked up, doing nothing by getting older, bitterer and more pissed off at the world? Or would you rather have a guy who served ten years of a fifteen-year sentence, but went through anger management, AA or NA, got his GED, and maybe learned a job skill? Which sounds better?"

Wilkins glanced at the Captain, his lower lip jutting like a sea bass. "You may have something . . . ." he started, but the radio interrupted. It was a long tone, a Code 1. "All units, Code 1, Unit 10, Code 1, Unit 10. Responders, acknowledge."

"Oak 18 and Oak 63, responding," the Captain said, and the radio crackled "Oak 62." That was Officer Sandy Hoover, another of the grounds patrol officers. She'd likely get there first, but she'd wait for direction from the captain before going in. Wilkins turned on the flashers and stepped on the gas. Inmates along the road turned to watch as they sped past.

"Control to responders, it's a live one!" the radio blared. The Captain's walkie-talkie was set to scan, and the channel in Unit 10 stayed open until the alarm was clear. He could hear the soft, Hispanic inflections of Sgt. Richard Alvarez talking to an inmate: "Man, you need to calm down. This doesn't have to be a big thing."

"Fuck you, Motherfucker," the inmate screamed. "I'll kick yoe ass! I'm sick of you people messin' with me with all your petty-ass bullshit rules! I done told you befoe, I aint gonna live with that fag no moe! If I gots to hurt you or anyone else to get out of here, I'll do what I gots to do!"

Wilkins pressed harder on the gas, and the van charged up the road between the housing units. Sgt. Alvarez, a sixty-year-old Texas-born Army veteran, ran a good unit and rarely had problems. But some Black inmates disliked taking orders from "a Mexican" — never mind that Alvarez had never been out of the country, much less to Mexico.

At the intersection, the Captain looked both ways. "Clear!" he said, and the van leapt through without stopping. Oak 62's car sat in front of the unit; Officer Hoover was waiting by the front door. The Captain ducked his head and was out of the van almost before it stopped moving. "Sandy," the Captain directed, "You take the side door, Wilkins will take the rear door and I'll go through the front!" He sprinted to the front door, as Wilkins and Hoover ran where the Captain had told them.

From the booth, Sgt. Alvarez was watching a lone inmate pace the dayroom, apparently cursing. "Edwards asked for a room change," Alvarez said, as Wilkins slipped opposite the Captain by the dayroom door. Hoover came in through the side door and stood off to the side, watching the hallway. "He doesn't like his celly, and I told him I couldn't move him without your approval. He started to go off on me and tried to come through the office window. I shut it and hit my body alarm."

The Captain strained to hear what the inmate was saying. He was as tall as a basketball player and as wide as a tackle, and his face held a mixture of pain and rage. "What's his first name?" The Captain asked, stepping out into the dayroom.

"Joshua," Alvarez called.

"Joshua, you need to calm down," the Captain said, approaching slowly. "What's happening?"

"That man always be messin with me!" Joshua yelled.

"How's that?" the Captain asked, as Hoover and Wilkins moved behind Joshua. She was about as tall as Wilkins, though he had her by about one hundred pounds, and she was the first woman on the institution SWAT team, a position she earned because she was good, dependable, and knew how to handle herself after years of Karate training.

"Man, I done told him I don' wanna be celled-up with no fag! He tol' me he ain't movin' me and I just better get used to it! I tol' him, 'That's bullshit,' and he tol' me to leave the office. When I tried to talk to him, he shut the window on my hand! That aint right! I went back up there an' he tol' me to go to my cell. I tol' him, 'Fuck that, if you aint gonna move me, I'll do what I gots to do!' Then he pressed the button an you all's showed up! I ain't goin' to no hole! You all's gonna have to fight me!" As he spoke, Joshua backed toward the wall, so that Monroe and Wilkins couldn't circle behind him.

"Joshua, you know I can't let you stay in here, " the Captain said. "I want you to turn around, face the wall, and put your hands behind your back, palms together." Monroe and Wilkins were within a couple leaping steps of him, almost close enough.

"Fuck that! I done tol' you, you all's gonna have to fight me!" Joshua screamed, squaring off to face the Captain. He took a couple of steps forward, and Hoover and Wilkins moved with him, flanking him.

The Captain's hands came up — he was only two steps from the burly inmate. "Joshua I'm not fighting you," he said, backing up. Through his shoulder mic', he called in the cavalry: "Oak 18 to Oak 23. Bring chemicals and the Taser to Unit 10 immediately. I have a resistant inmate. Oak 18 to additional responders, 10-25 Unit 10."

"10-4, Oak 18, 23 responding." In the next ten seconds, three more patrols crackled their response.

"Joshua, you aren't going to win," the Captain said. "I've got at least three more patrols and a lieutenant coming down with gas and a taser. If that doesn't work, there'll be more guys coming. You're going to get yourself hurt, and if you hurt anyone else, you'll get yourself a new case. Turn around, and I'll cuff you, and no one gets hurt."

"It aint right!" Joshua sobbed, his big shoulders heaving. "It just aint right!" He threw his hands in the air, his shoulders slumped, and he lowered his head, tears streaming down his cheeks. He turned toward the wall and put his hands behind his back. Wilkins and Monroe moved in quickly, each taking hold of an arm, while the Captain snapped on the cuffs, enlarging them to the biggest ratchet. Joshua's wrists were so large, the Captain was relieved they'd close at all.

"You're doing the right thing," he told the sobbing man. "We're going to take you to seg., and I'll get your statement there."

"It just ain't right," Joshua sniffed. "It just aint right."

Inmates along the roadway strained to see who was in the back of the van, behind the tinted windows. Looking at his lap, Joshua cried all the way to seg..

As Officer Jones removed Joshua's handcuffs through the trap in the strip cell, and long, wrenching cries filled the air as the big man fought to catch his breath. "People always be fuckin' with me!" he wailed. "Why don' they just leave me alone? Why they always gots to be fuckin' with me?"

The Captain approached the slit window. "Joshua, you need to calm down. Right now, things seem pretty bad, but no one got hurt, you followed all my orders, and if you don't cause any trouble up here, you'll be out in a few days. You'll be moving to a different unit once you get cut out of Seg., so just chill out for a while. Follow the officer's directions. We have to do a strip search. "

"Fuck that! I ain't lettin' no one look up my ass!"

"Joshua, you've been doing well. Don't get yourself wrapped up in more trouble." The Captain leaned over to Officer Jones. "I'll do the strip search." He put his face to the window. "Is that OK with you, Joshua?"

"OK," he said meekly.

"Let's get it done then. Joshua, hand your clothes out through the trap, and we'll get the search done and get you to a cell." The Captain pulled on a sticky pair of latex rubber gloves. "I've got a doctor coming up to talk to you, but he won't see you until you're in a cell. Let's go."

Joshua handed his clothes through the slot in the door, and the Captain searched each article. "Run your fingers through your hair," he said when Joshua was naked. "Show me behind each ear." Joshua's sobs faded, as he moved through the ritual. "Open your mouth and lift your tongue. Turn your lip back. Good. Now, spread your fingers and put your hands over your head." The inmate's round face relaxed and his breathing came evenly. "Turn around so I can see your armpits. All, right, lift your sack. OK, turn around and show me the bottoms of your feet. Good, now bend over, spread you cheeks and cough. All right, Joshua, what size underwear and jumpsuit do you want?"

"Could I have a 4X?" he asked, "and I wear a size sixteen shoe." It never ceased to amaze the Captain how quickly some inmates could relax once the spasms of resistance were spent and the routines were flowing — even routines as humiliating as a strip-search.

Once dressed, Joshua put his hands through the trap in the door, and the Captain fitted him with a larger set of handcuffs. "Open strip cell," he said into his radio, and he took the big man by the arm. "We're going to put you in cell forty-nine. The doctor is here, and he'll see you as soon as you're settled in. You doing OK, Big Guy?"

"Ya, Cap, I'm OK now." Joshua gave a little shudder, an echo of the sobs that had rocked him all the way to Seg. "I'm OK."

"You're doing fine, Joshua," the Captain said. "Thank you."

When the cuffs were removed, Joshua went to the back of his cell and looked out the small window into the main rec. yard, where inmates were jogging or walking on the track. From the hall, the Captain could their laughter and friendly shouts. Joshua's shoulders began to shake as he watched at the window. Quietly, he wiped tears off of his cheeks. No matter how big a man is the Captain thought, loneliness and isolation makes him small.

"I wonder what he's in for," Wilkins said as they left Seg.

"Whatever it is," the Captain said, "he hurts just like anyone."

CHAPTER VII

The door to the office slammed open, and Leon Nelson strutted in, his burn-scarred head held high, a conquering warrior. He glared at the Captain, a sneer contorting his already deformed face. "Well, lookey-here," he said, as though he were surprised to see him, "you sure ain't such hot-shit now, is you? Sittin' there all messed up, yer pretty white shirt all tore-up and bloody. You ain't shit, mother-fucker." He leaned in close and whispered, "It's about you and me, mother-fucker, just you and me!" Leaning back, he cleared his nose with a harsh sniff, then rumbled his throat clear and spit in the Captain's face. "That's all you gonna be gettin' from me, mother-fucker. That and a knife in your throat."

The Captain leaned to wipe the spit on the shoulder of his shirt. "Leon," he said, "if it's about us, why don't you let these other people go, and we'll settle it, just the two of us? There isn't any need for anyone else to get hurt."

"Fuck them," Leon said. "If'n they gets hurt, it's on your head, not mine."

"No, Leon. You started this and whatever happens is on your head" The Captain shook his head, as though they doing nothing riskier than negotiating the price of a used car, and a pesky spouse was muddying the deal. "Let it really be between you and me."

Leon squared his lean shoulders and looked at the Captain, as though thinking it over, then, fast as a lizard catching a bug, slammed

a fist into the Captain's side. The already cracked ribs gave, and with a
"pop!" another couple snapped. The pain took his breath away.

"There you go mother-fucker. That's for what YOU started when
you threw me in the hole! That's for what you started when you pulled
me out a that fucken' fire! You just remember who's calling the shots
now. "Q," Leon said, as he left the room, "if he causes any trouble, you
call and I'll take care of it mysef."

* * *

11:38 a.m.

"HEY, CAP," WILKINS SAID. "YOU remember Douglas?
Now there was an example of rehabilitation!"

The Captain's stomach was beginning to rumble, but they'd
decided to visit one more unit before lunch. Wilkins was steering
the van toward Unit Fifteen, the "program unit". It was there that
inmates were in a program for either drug or sex offenses, and
many times, a combination of the two. "How could I forget such
a success story?" he said. JuWayne Douglas was what the security
staff called a "Program Junkie." When the Captain had first met
him, more than twenty years ago, he had been involved in a
"Transactional Analysis" program. In T.A., Douglas was supposed
to get in touch with his "inner-child" and resolve the anger he
had built up over time. He was also in Narcotics Anonymous,
Alcoholics Anonymous, Bible Study, Anger Management and
one-on-one counseling. Douglas excelled in every program he
entered, and the social workers and Treatment people treated
him almost like staff. He was a mentor to other inmates and a
spokesman for the local version of "Scared Straight."

If you asked, Douglas would tell you he was in because of
drugs. He admitted to robbing upwards of fifteen houses, all
while the people were home. He was, in his own words, "a one-
man crime wave." But that was all behind him. He had turned his

life around. You see, he was in love. He'd met a woman through a "lonely hearts" add in a local newspaper:

"Thirty-two-year-old repressed five-foot-ten, one hundred seventy-five pound Black Warrior is in need of a Princess. Am college educated, independent, and looking for someone special. If you're special, or want to be treated special, write to..."

Within a week, Douglas had a dozen replies, most of them with photos. He read through them all, and the one that caught his eye was from Alicia, an overweight, rather unattractive single mother who, by her own description, had spent too much of her life being kicked around and was ready to feel special. Douglas knew he could make Alicia feel special.

He sent her a letter and photos every day for two weeks, explaining that he was in prison for stealing to support a drug habit. He told of his undying love for his mother, who had passed on five years ago, and he confessed that, at first, only drugs had killed the pain of the loss. He told her he was using prison to become a better person, though the guards were cruel and racist, and the food and routine were dull almost beyond endurance. She had changed that, though, becoming the beacon that gave his life meaning. He lived and died for her.

Alicia wrote as often as he did. He made her feel special. She loved him. He was her reason for being. She visited, and was heavier than in her pictures, but she dressed nicely and bought him cigarettes and soda out of the vending machines in the visitors' room. She didn't like seeing him in prison greens, so she sent him a couple of pair of Levi's, a couple of shirts, and a pair of Nike's. She sent twenty-five dollars a week to his canteen account. After a month or two, she sent him a radio, then a thirteen-inch color TV.

She finally introduced him to her nine-year-old daughter, Candy, who had never really had a father. It wasn't too long before she was sitting on his lap during visits, calling him "Daddy." On Father's Day, Candy sent him a card, and Douglas sent Alicia Mother's Day cards and remembered both of their birthdays.

Christmas was a time of wonder for them all. Douglas made sure that Candy received presents through the Salvation Army, and he bought presents for his lady-love out of the canteen account that she kept flush. They were all happy, and Douglas was the happiest of them all. Never in his life had he had someone to love. Never in his life had he had someone who cared for him and respected him. Never in his life had he had someone buy him things, asking nothing in return. They were married in the prison chapel.

Alicia wrote to the Parole Board, telling of their love for each other, and what a wonderful father Douglas had become to Candy, whom he planned to adopt. A photo included the letter showed Douglas standing between Candy, now twelve years old, and Alicia, with an arm around each as they looked up lovingly at his smiling face.

Douglas had been turned down for parole every year for the past seventeen years, but he now had a job waiting for him in a self-help program, letters in his file from the North Woods warden, as well as a chaplain, a social worker, and three staff psychologists, and his wife. His disciplinary record was clean, and he'd even been accepted into college.

The Parole Board noted what Alicia hadn't bothered to check: that Douglas was a sexual predator, serving a twenty-five-year term for three violent rapes committed while robbing those houses. He had beaten one young victim nearly to death, and another, years later, had committed suicide. As a juvenile, he had raped his sister and a young cousin. His mother — not dead, as Alicia thought — had cut Douglas off after he was found guilty of his sister's rape. The only prison program he'd never taken was the Sex Offender Treatment Program.

Yet, when faced with all that he Douglas done to rehabilitate himself, the Parole Board saw no other recourse than to grant a parole. Douglas, Alicia, and Candy were ecstatic! In a month, they would begin their life together as a family.

At eight o'clock in the morning on the big day, Alicia and Candy arrived wearing new dresses. Douglas met them at the gate, wearing a new three-piece suit that Alicia had sent. The three of them climbed into the front seat of Alicia's ten-year-old Chevy sedan, and what happened next is murky.

What is known is that Douglas's new wife drove to the nearest ATM and withdrew seven hundred and fifty dollars, then headed toward Chicago with Douglas and his Candy in the back seat. Between North Woods Correctional Institution and Milwaukee, Douglas had Alicia pull off on a side road and drive about five miles from the highway, where they all got out of the car. Douglas punched Alicia in the face, shattering her nose and teeth. While she lay bleeding and moaning, he raped his new daughter. Then he raped Alicia. He took the money and the car, and left them — bleeding, beaten, and half naked — at the edge of a corn field.

A farmer came across them around sunset. By that time, Douglas had a good six-hour lead. He stopped to see his mother, but she wouldn't let him in her door. She called the police, but my then, he was on his way out of town. Police caught up with him at a motel outside of Chicago in the morning. Alicia's car was in the parking lot. Douglas had checked in to room 103. There was no answer when they knocked, so they got the key from the front desk and found Douglas hanging from a shower rod.

"At least he's rehabilitated and won't be another recidivism statistic," Wilkins said, "but it's too bad he didn't rehabilitate himself on the shower rod before he got out. I never heard what happened to the wife and daughter. Don't ya ever wonder why some of these women get hooked up with an inmate?"

"I do," the Captain said, thinking of Wilkins's sister all those years ago, bleeding out from a knife wound, in the parking lot of a night club. She hadn't gotten mixed up with an inmate or any jerk. She just got unlucky.

"Well," Wilkins said, "I think it has to do with a couple of things. For one thing, if you get mixed up with an inmate, you sure as Hell know where he's going to be every night. You don't have to worry that he's sleeping with the babysitter. And you don't have to worry that he's getting in trouble on the street; he has the equivalent of police protection twenty-four-seven.

"Then there's the control thing. A woman with an inmate for a boyfriend is in control. He depends on her for money, and he knows she's free to look elsewhere if she wants. He can't make her visit or write if she's mad at him. She doesn't have to accept his phone calls. She's free."

The Captain shrugged. "But what about the ones that stick around once a guy gets out? I guess maybe they hope that they've changed him. Everybody wants to make made a difference. Is that it?"

Wilkins nodded. "I also think it's the "bad boy" thing. Women are attracted by the outlaw image and the element of danger. They don't think about the path of victims left behind." Wilkins slowed the van. "All I know is, any woman that hooks up with one of these guys is asking for trouble. Where you wanna' eat?"

CHAPTER VIII

The Captain slumped forward in his chair to ease the pain. He was sure that a couple of his ribs were broken. He'd broken ribs before, when he was a wrestler in high school, and he was familiar with the pain he was feeling, remembering it from over thirty years ago.

"You jes sit there," Q-Ball said, leaning forward in his chair.

The Captain took a couple of deep breaths and straightened, and Q-ball slouched back in his chair, his legs splayed out in a comfortable "V." "Tha's nice," Q-ball said, with a sinister smile.

The broken ribs hadn't punctured his lungs, the Captain realized, and the pain was tolerable. He had lost his glasses in the fighting, but his vision was good enough to see what was going on through the window in the office door. The inmates were busy out there: piling bunk beds as barriers to the side doors, spreading liquid soap on the floors by the front and kitchen entrances, fashioning weapons out of everything from mop handles to what looked like toothbrushes with razor blades melted into the handles. They hadn't touched the video cameras in plexiglass bubbles on the ceiling, so there was no doubt that the Control Center was watching their preparations. The SWAT team would be ready in a matter of minutes, the Captain figured, as would the negotiators — and snipers were probably already covering the exits to Unit Fifteen. The Captain had trained the eight men on the sniper team, and trusted each one. They worked in teams of two, one on the rifle, the other observing range, wind, and angle for an accurate shot — and relaying information to Thorson. Everyone was busy, the Captain thought, except the hostages.

All he could do was sit in the chair and looked around the dingy office. Desk, computer, and two empty chairs — not much to work with: the window was covered by bars and the only door out led into the unit, where Leon Nelson's minions were readying for war.

Years ago, Nelson's threats had seemed no more than empty words, the kind of raging nonsense that built an officer's emotional armor. Now, Nelson was in command of Unit Fifteen, and the Captain was more scared than he had ever been in his life. He had no illusion that Leon would let him live. If he wanted to see Maura and the girls again, he would need to call on every ounce of his wit, patience, strength, and wisdom — and no small measure of luck.

*   *   *

11:40am

"WHAT'S FOR LUNCH, ANYWAY?"

"It's burger day," Wilkins said, as he pulled to a stop at the V-shaped Unit Fifteen. "Bergman will have enough for us. He always does." They exited the van, no bumps or scrapes, and walked up the steps into the rear of the unit. The Captain queried "I wonder what Bergman's up to,"

"It's always something, isn't it?" Wilkins laughed as they pushed through the door into the largest unit in the prison.

There were two hundred and fifty inmates of Unit Fifteen and all were enrolled in either a drug program or sex offender program. Most were grand-fathered in under the "old law." Under the old law, they had to finish two-thirds of their sentence and if they weren't a problem they were released. If they completed a program, they could be considered for release at the half-way point. So if they finished their programs, they had a chance of getting out early. IF they finished the program successfully. If they "flunked out," they would have to serve their complete sentence. They had lots of staff to help them succeed— half a dozen social workers, two officers and Sgt. Bergman.

Bergman, blond and buff, with steely blue eyes, stood at his desk, gesticulating like an exasperated symphony conductor at a stocky Hispanic inmate. "I don't know what's the matter with the washing machine, Charles. It's broken so you can't use it. Maintenance will be here tomorrow."

"What am I supposed to do for clean clothes?" The inmate spread his arms as though to display his shabbiness. He looked pretty sharp, as far as the Captain could tell, in creased jeans and a spotless white t-shirt.

"You can either wash them by hand or wear the one's you have on. You'll get clean greens at laundry exchange tonight."

"You know I don't wear that State crap," Charles said.

"Well, you'll have to wear State crap for today, Charles," Bergman said, sinking into his chair, slicing the air.

"I'm filing a complaint!" Charles murmured. "You can't make me wear dirty clothes!"

"No one is making you wear dirty clothes, Charles. If you don't want to wear the clothes the State provides, it's your choice to wear dirty clothes." Bergman hung his head, suddenly defeated. Charles shook his head sadly, and left. Wilkins coughed into his fist, and Bergman jumped.

"Oh, it's you guys. How do you like Charles? He was a doctor before he got caught molesting little kids, so he thinks he's got something coming."

"Sorry about the washing machine, man," Wilkins said, straddling a chair.

Bergman shrugged. "I put a sign on it saying it's broken, but I'll bet at least twelve dumb-asses went and tried it and came to me: 'Is the washer broke?' If you'd let me put up my Ebonics sign, nobody would bother me."

"Sarge, you better not have that sign anywhere in this Unit!" the Captain said, suppressing a smile. The last time the washer broke, Bergman had gotten so tired of inmates asking what was wrong with it that he'd left a new sign:

Washin' cheen boken! Don't Axe!

"The amazing thing," Bergman said, "is that with that sign, *nobody* asked!

"It was hardly appropriate," the Captain said.

"Or maybe it was entirely appropriate," Bergman said. "Why make them speak the Queen's English, when they have a perfectly serviceable dialect?" For the last four years, Bergman had used two weeks of his vacation to travel to Africa, at his own expense, and help villagers build houses and churches. His team from church had brought soap, toothbrushes, tennis shoes, shorts, t-shirts, and other basics, and they'd taught hygiene, the three "r's" and Bible studies. Though he had two daughters in college, Bergman somehow managed to tithe to the project. He'd come down with a case of Malaria so bad, during his first visit, that he had to be medevac'd to a hospital and spend two weeks in intensive care. He couldn't wait to go back.

Bergman picked up a photo of a smiling brunette and waved it at them. "Genevieve, my oldest, is bringing her boyfriend home this weekend, and she said he has something to ask me."

"He wants to marry her?" the Captain said. "What are you going to tell him?" Bergman hadn't allowed his daughters to date until they were out of High School, and if the Captain remembered right, this was only Genevieve's second boyfriend.

"He's scared to death of me," Bergman said, "so I guess if he's got guts enough to ask, I'll have to say yes." Bergman was the toughest man the Captain knew. He'd grown up the third of eight brothers, watching out in both directions. Though he rarely worked-out, he was solid muscle. On the North Woods SWAT Team, he was always the first man through the door. It was undoubtedly an act of bravery to ask Bergman for his daughter's hand. "He's studying for the Foreign Mission field, the same as Genevieve," Bergman said. "He's got a good heart. I think he'll make a good husband."

"I pity the guy if he doesn't," the Captain laughed.

"You got that right! The first time I met him I asked if he had good health and fire insurance, because you never know when you may need it. Genevieve told him she *thought* I was only joking, but she couldn't be sure. It'll take him a while to figure me out."

"I don't know, Sarge," the Captain said. "I've known you for the better part of fifteen years, and I haven't figured you out. Are you taking the promotional exam next month?"

"I dunno. The last time I took it, I scored so low, I was afraid they were going to reclassify me as a moron. I'm not a good test taker. I'd like to promote, but I ain't counting on it."

"You'd make a good supervisor. You've got common sense. People look up to you. I'd enjoy having you in the office."

Officer Mark Zielke, tall and lean, came striding up the hallway from a cell, followed by a slight, coffee-colored inmate who was wringing his hands. Damn, Zielke, why you always be bustin' my ass?" the inmate said.

Zielke held a small bag under his arm. "Damn, Webster," he said over his shoulder, "why do you always make it so easy to bust your ass? You know the rules, and yet every time I search your room, I find something! Whose radio is this?"

"Man, it belonged to Dude!" Webster slapped his hands to his cheeks. "He went home last week an' he jes left it in the cell! I figured I might jes as well use it."

Zielke rolled his eyes. "Well, it's not yours, so now you're getting a write-up."

Webster turned to the Captain, shaking his head sadly. "Man, Cap! I can't afford no more write-ups! If'n you jes takes the radio, ain't that enough?"

"Cap," Zielke said, "every time I check his cell, he has something he shouldn't. Last week, he had a loaf of bread and a jar of peanut butter he stole out of the unit kitchen. Before that, he had someone else's shoes and shirt. I can't go in his room without finding something!"

"Webster," the Captain said, "you know Officer Zielke is going to find something if you have it. Why do you keep playing games with him?"

"I ain't playin' no games! I jes be gettin' stuff all the time. An' eve'ytime I gets me somethin', Zielke be findin' it!"

"The way I see it, Webster, Officer Zielke is doing his job. Knock the crap off, and Officer Zielke won't have to be finding stuff. The next time he writes you up, I'll put you in seg., where you can't be gettin' nothin'. Understand?"

"Yeah, Cap, I understands." Webster looked at his feet like a kid caught with his brother's Halloween candy.

"You head back to whatever you had going," the Captain said. Webster shuffled away, looking once over his shoulder and shaking his head at Zielke.

"He's okay," Zielke said, "but he's got to kick that habit or he'll get shivved."

Officer Terry Zielke had spent eleven years in the Navy before moving to the Midwest for a marriage that failed. He was used to everything being in its place.

His partner, Officer Gary Dern, came up the hall, heading for the kitchen. Dern had spent seven years in the Marine Corps but looked like he had gotten out yesterday. The two partners bickered constantly about which branch of the service was the best. "Mornin', Cap," Dern said. "Eating lunch here today?"

"I guess so," the Captain said, "if you two old women will quit bickering long enough for me to enjoy it!"

"Well, if the old Pier Queer would just lay-off, I sure wouldn't be starting anything," Dern said.

"Cap," Zielke said, "you hear they compared the average IQ of a Marine to an idiot, and there's only a five point difference? The idiots are upset; they say the Marines cheated to get that close!"

NO PLACE LIKE HOME

It didn't really matter who started it: either way it was going to get started. During one exchange, Zielke had reminded Dern, "Remember, the Marines are a Department of the Navy," to which Dern had replied, "That's right. The Men's department!" Zielke had gotten back at him by asking Dern why there were Marines — he called them "bullet catchers" — on ships. "For security," Dern had said, to which Zielke had replied, "Oh, I thought it was so the sailors had someone to dance with." Thus it went. Yet, for all of their arguing, they knew they could depend on each other, and the Captain knew he could depend on them. They, too, were a part of the SWAT team.

In the kitchen, the Captain and Wilkins were served the same food as the inmates: Today it was BLT's, steak fries, green beans, and peach cobbler. A couple of the inmate kitchen workers fussed over the Captain, hoping for an "in" with him should they catch a case later on, and threw a few extra slices of bacon on the sandwich, but the smart ones knew it didn't matter: they'd get treated the same as everyone, no matter how they fussed in the kitchen.

"Hi 'ya, Captain! How's it goin'?" asked an old con who was cutting up the cobbler.

"As long as they keep paying me for this, it's going great!" The Captain grinned. "Williams," he said looking at the man's name tag, "where do I know you from?"

Williams laughed. "Man, you gassed my ass and thumped me pretty good a few years ago. I was actin' out some shit, and you took care o' biddness. You was fair, and I deserved it! If I'd o' had any brains when I was young, I'd be doin' what you are." A couple of the younger kitchen workers eyed Williams, suspicious of his friendliness with the "Po-lice." He flapped a hand at one and shook his head; his monolog was aimed as much at them as it was at the Captain.

"Yeah, it's a pretty good deal," the Captain said. "They feed me, they give me clothes to wear, and then they pay me. What brings you back here?"

"I got eight more to do on a twenty-year bit," Williams said, "but this is the last time you'll ever see me. I been jailin' since I was seventeen. I got my ass kicked so many times I felt like there was a waitin' line or somethin'. But the last time I was out, I hooked up with a woman. We got married and had us a couple o' kids. I had me a payin' job, an' I thought eveythin' was OK. Then I saw me an easy score. I done got busted for bein' stupid. My wife done left me, I ain't seen or heard from my kids in six years, an' I can't remember the last time I had me a letter or a visit."

The young inmates listened as Williams spoke. Some laughed, others looked away uneasily, their future revealed.

"Yessir, Cap, when I get out, you ain't never gonna see me again! I be tired of this shit."

"I hope you're right, and I hope your time goes well. It's good to see you, Man." The Captain thought of the hundreds of inmates who had made the same vow, yet back they came. For many, prison life was all they knew. They had grown up in institutions and were used to others making decisions for them. They didn't have to think about what time to get up or go to bed, what to have for meals, or how to budget their money. They didn't have to worry about kids, car insurance, house payments, or going to the doctor. It was all taken care of. Some had lost everything when they first came to prison. They had no family or friends, except in prison.

Wilkins and the Captain took their food trays and sat at the sergeant's desk. All around them, inmates were checking in from work or school or checking out for the infirmary, the dentist, or the property department. Life in prison didn't stop for lunch.

CHAPTER IX

Officers Kyle Hennricks and Phil Adams sat on the floor across the room from the captain. Their black t-shirts were ripped and torn, hanging in them by a few threads. The handcuffs from their own belts held their hands helpless in front of them, and the inmates had stripped the equipment from their duty belts. They stared vacantly at the floor, avoiding any appearance of challenging Q-ball. Kyle Hennricks was twenty-one and today was his first day after training. "It will likely be his last," the Captain couldn't help thinking. "Even if he lives, who's going to want to come back?" Adams was a couple of years older than the Captain and had been, before Wilkins, the Captain's right-hand man. The Captain couldn't tell if either of them had been injured in the takeover, but he knew that things would get a lot worse, and he silently prayed they would all make it through.

Q-Ball stood silently by the door, his eyes traveling sternly from one captive to the next, but the Captain could see that he, too, was afraid. 'If we have nothing else in common,' the Captain thought, 'at least we share fear.' With Golden — wherever she was— the inmates had at least four bargaining chips. Because the Captain was the highest ranking, the inmates would assume him to be more valuable. The truth was, all rank evaporated in such a situation. The administrative hot shots were probably crapping their pants, worrying about how the crisis would affect their careers. The warden, who had never worked a day of security in her life, was probably wishing she were back in her old job, running the commissary. Thorson was no doubt strutting around issuing orders like Mussolini with O'Malley hot on his tail, ready to approve any decision he may have. The Captain took no comfort in the thought of them. But he knew that as his world was falling to pieces, the hostage rescue team, people he had trained and worked with, were gearing up, and preparing for battle. Bergman, Murphy, Dern, Zielke, Murphy Warinski, Hoover: these, he trusted. Each would be donning black combat uniforms, lightweight stab vests, and knee and elbow pads. They would be stuffing their pockets with flash-bang grenades, nylon flex-cuffs, extra magazines for the assault rifles, and, in Bergman and Murphy's cases, extra shells for twelve gauge shotguns. They would be checking their duty belts: Beretta pistol, two extra magazines, OC pepper-spray, batons, gas mask and flip-blade knife. Roland Halfbeck, as the team leader, would carry an M-79 grenade launcher. The team would fire gas and flash-bangs into the building, and Sergeants Murphy and Bergman would greet anyone who blocked their way with a blast of twelve-gauge 00 buckshot. The team would shoot those inmates who resisted and cuff those who didn't. They would rush the hostages to safety, then care for injured or dead inmates. Ideally, that is.

The Captain knew that his snipers, too, would be gathering their tools of death. They had sighted in and practiced long hours, twice a month, with their Remington 700 rifles, and now they would be setting them on bi-pods, calculating range, weather and wind. Their main responsibility: Kill anyone who tried to hurt the hostages. During training, each sniper could, at four hundred yards and in less than five seconds, place three shots in a circle the size of a penny. They knew how to shoot for the sweet spot between a person's upper lip and nose, stopping any reaction, effectively severing and blowing away the brain stem. They knew not to hesitate. They knew of the nightmares they'd suffer afterwards, and the guilt they'd feel for taking a person's life. They knew life would never be the same; they might wallow in pity and guilt or find gratitude for the lives they had saved and the days remaining to them. It was different for each man, and each had prepared in his own way. Dealing death was a serious business.

* * *

12:02pm

"DAVE, CAN YOU TAKE ME up front?" the Captain said as he and Wilkins cleaned off their trays. "I've got to go talk to one of your union thugs." On the way to the car, he took a last gulp of Diet Coke and threw the bottle in the garbage. He ducked, climbing into the van, and said a prayer of thanks that he'd remembered to save his scalp. Wilkins stuffed a fresh chew under his lip.

"Radio me when you're done," Wilkins said, dropping him. "While you're busy, I'm gonna go try to repair my reputation"

"Good luck with that." The Captain replied as he walked to his office. Entering, he grabbed a sheaf of notes from his desk, grabbed a fresh, cold Diet Coke from the refrigerator in the office and made his way to the meeting room. He took a long pull on the bottle, feeling the same satisfaction as a drunk with a good Scotch. He knew the bullshit to follow would put him close to the edge, and he'd take his comfort where he could. Barry Wink, the union president, sat at a long table talking with Officer Winslow. He looked like a fat Jethro BoDean gone to seed. Wink and the Captain had a history, and it wasn't a good one.

Wink's wife, Gloria, had worked at the prison for a while, and the Captain had written her up for dereliction of duty. She'd been working the main control center and had screwed-up the count board so bad that the count was off by more than 10 inmates. The mistake was because she refused to put all of the inmate transfers for the day on the board, and when the Captain told her to straighten it out, she refused. He told her three times, and after the last refusal, he removed her from the post. She was given a disciplinary write-up, but before it could be done, she was so mad, she quit. The Captain considered it a blessing; Wink resented it because his wife never got another job, and he had to work overtime. In the Captain's mind, Wink was about as useful as a one-armed trapeze performer with an itchy ass. He'd gotten elected union president more because he was a load-mouth than anything else.

Union Steward Tom Peterson sat across from Wink and Winslow. He was lean and fit, a weight lifter, and he moved with the crisp, tough swagger of John Wayne. The number-one senior officer, now that Pinky was gone, he worked in Admin' and often reminded new officers, "I have more time on the shitter than you have in uniform." He and the Captain had a working relationship, though it ended there. Peterson was a union man through and through, and as such, considered the Captain an adversary. The Captain respected Peterson's position, tolerated his occasional pomposity, and marveled each time he fought a petty grievance.

Winslow's grievance against the Captain — for missing his name when making calls to fill a third-shift overtime position — was lame. The way overtime worked was that an Officer signed up for the shift he wanted and was called based on seniority. Often, twenty or thirty Officers signed up, though only three or four wanted an overtime shift. The rest signed up in hopes of being overlooked. Then they could file a grievance, which would allow them to work the overtime when they wanted. The local agreement gave them a month to make up the overtime, and they could schedule an hour or two a day. The agreement also specified that the only place grievance overtime could be worked was in the mailroom. The whole system, in the Captain's opinion, stunk.

Winslow was a weasel. He signed up for overtime every shift, every day. The Captain couldn't remember the last time he had accepted any, but Winslow checked the books every day to see if he was missed. Grievance overtime meant that he could sit in the mailroom, drink coffee, and read magazines under the guise of sorting mail. The mailroom officers didn't want outsiders touching the mail and screwing with their system, so in their view, the less the slouches did the better. The Captain had been down there on days when there were two or three extra officers on make-up overtime all sitting around, having a nice little tea party.

Overtime, as a whole, was out of hand. Some Officers worked two sixteen-hour shifts, followed by a regular shift, then two more sixteens. While some had to be ordered to take extra shifts, others were "OT Dogs," earning so much overtime that they made more money than the warden. One transportation officer worked an average of one hundred and twenty hours of overtime each pay period. He worked double shifts whenever he could, including on his weekends. He took a cell-phone with him when he camped at a local campground so he could call and see what was available for OT. Never mind that his sixteen-year-old son had been arrested four times for under-age drinking and three times for disorderly conduct and that his wife had left him on a number of occasions. Never mind that he smoked three packs of cigarettes a day, and as he approached the age of sixty, had no intention of retiring. Never mind that he was just as "institutionalized" as any lifer. He was the highest paid security staff in the entire State Department of Corrections.

Wink cleared his throat and gestured at the Captain to take a seat. "Officer Winslow was signed up for second-shift overtime on Saturday," he began." He says he wasn't called, and Officer Stinson, who has less seniority, took the overtime."

The Captain consulted his notes. "Last Saturday, I had to fill nineteen positions on second shift. Fourteen Officers from third shift were already working double shifts and weren't eligible. Only seven sergeants had signed up for OT, and twenty officers. The officer positions went right away, but no one wanted to work the sergeant jobs in the housing units. Winslow was eligible to work sergeant overtime, provided no sergeant took the overtime." The Captain could not recall Winslow ever working a housing unit. "According to the call-in sheet, I placed a call to Officer Winslow's house at 12:23 p.m. There was no answer after nineteen rings."

"That's impossible!" Winslow said. "I was home all day."

"Well, that's what the record shows. Is this your phone number?" the Captain shoved the OT record across the table.

"Yeah, that's my number, but I still don't think you called."

"Officer Winslow, I have no reason to lie about it. As it was, I had to order a number of people to stay for sixteen-hour shifts. What makes you think I wouldn't call you?"

Winslow turned to Peterson. "I know I wasn't called! I was home all afternoon."

"Is it possible that you were busy with something and didn't hear the phone?" the Captain asked.

"No. I was in the house and the phone didn't ring!"

"Well, I don't know what to tell you. The record shows that I tried to call your house and there was no answer. If you want me to, I can get a print-out from the institution phone log. I don't know why you didn't get the call, but the call was made." The whole thing was ridiculous. All four men knew that Winslow wouldn't have accepted the overtime anyway. It was just a game for easy money. It was sad that the union went along with it.

The Captain had once been a union official at North Woods. He'd started as a shift steward and progressed to chief steward at a time when the local was militant, management was uncommunicative, and neither side had any respect for the other. The union had urged members to wear white tennis shoes instead of their black uniform shoes to protest management recalcitrance on a host of issues which they summed up as failure to treat them as professionals. The Captain had realized the irony and opposed the plan: showing up like a bunch of Bozos in their white shoes, they'd essentially betrayed their professionalism. After a while it had become painfully obvious that he was expected to defend guilty people who deserved to lose their job. The final straw came when dope was found in a tower.

A new officer, fresh from the academy, checked everything as he began his shift in the tower. The rifle and shotgun were in their racks, each with two boxes of extra shells. The semi-auto pistol was in the holster underneath them. The binoculars, walkie-talkie, and telephone were in working order. He was about to slide the floor-to-ceiling glass-door open to go out on the catwalk when, on a shelf next to the tower log, he found a small plastic bag containing a little box of stick matches, a metal pipe, and a small amount of pot. In the garbage, he found ashes and burnt stick matches.

The rookie called the shift commander. "I need you to come up to Tower four right away. I found something, and I think you need to see it."

Everyone knew to whom the pot belonged. The first shift officer was a stoner. Yet the union took up his cause.

"How can you prove he did it? Did you get fingerprints off of the pipe? Maybe the rookie is just trying to make a name for himself! Maybe he put it there as a set-up!" It went on and on.

The Captain was livid. "Here's a guy who is supposed to be protecting all of us. He's up there with a hi-powered rifle, higher than a kite. He was so high he forgot his bag! He's putting us at risk! Yet we're supposed to defend him? We're supposed to save his job! I'm sorry, but I won't. It's a bunch of B.S."

As it turned out, the Captain didn't have to defend him. The union president took it as a personal challenge to save the man's job. He went at it with a vengeance, attacking not only management but also the rookie.

The rookie transferred out when he started getting threatening phone calls at home labeling him a "management snitch."

In his resignation letter as steward, the Captain argued that when the union defended officers who should be fired, it was doing a disservice not only to itself but to the department. Two months later, when the hostility of the union leadership was clear, he too transferred — to the Meadow Creek Correctional Institution…the Meadows. Relations at the Meadows were a bit better. But in the Captain's mind, this local too went out of its way to protect those who didn't deserve protection — at the expense of those who did.

"Captain, I don't doubt that you tried to call Officer Winslow," Peterson said, "but we would like to see the call logs."

The Captain stood up. "I'll get them from the business office by tomorrow" he said, shaking hands with Peterson. After the door closed behind him, he could hear Winslow's whiny sing-song continuing to press his case. Poor Peterson; he wouldn't wish the job on anyone. The Captain took a last swig of his Coke and tossed it in a can as he headed to his office. He needed to spend some time on paperwork, which he hated, but somehow, as Winslow's whining faded behind him, he was happy at the prospect.

CHAPTER X

Q-Ball leaned on the door, scowling at the hostages.

"Are you guys all right?" the Captain asked.

"You shut the fuck up." Q-Ball straightened.

"Q-Ball, I just want to make sure that everyone is OK. As long as no one is hurt too badly, no one is in any real trouble."

"They be OK." Q-Ball grunted. "Go ahead an' talk to 'em, just don' be tryin' noffin'."

"Hennricks, how you doing?"

"I'm OK." Hennricks smiled. His black T-shirt was torn at the collar, and his arms showed a few scrapes and bruises, but even now, he projected the fresh-scrubbed look of a country boy. "You don't look so good, though."

"I've been better. It's not as bad as it looks, but it hurts like hell." That was an understatement; the Captain had never been in as much pain in his life. His entire face throbbed, and it felt as though someone were stabbing him in the side with a pitchfork every time he took a breath. They had allowed him to keep his white shirt, which was torn and blood-streaked. The left knee of his neatly-pressed trousers was ripped wide open.

"Man, Captain, they grabbed us from behind," Adams said. "We didn't have a chance to fight."

"It's probably better that way. At least you're not hurt. Where's the Sarge?"

Adams and Hennricks both shrugged. The separation of Sgt. Golden did not bode well for her. Tears welled in Hennricks's eyes. "We saw her get hit, and someone dragged her to the laundry room." The Captain had a vague recollection of seeing her dragged while he was fighting.

"How you doing, Phil?" the Captain asked.

"Kemo-Sabe, this is the worst fix you ever got us into!" Adams said with a slight smile. Adams had started in Corrections shortly after the Captain and never risen past the rank of officer. He was certainly intelligent enough, and his resume included service as a member of the SWAT team, but that was before his marriage dissolved and he dove into the bottle. He had recently returned to work after a heart attack. He wasn't much older than the Captain, but he was heavy, pale, and graying. Slumped in a chair with his hands cuffed, he looked as old as a nursing home resident.

Outside, it had quieted down. The initial adrenalin rush had subsided, and the inmates were starting to realize the gravity of what they had done. They were starting to separate into groups, gang-bangers in one area, skinheads in another, those simply caught up in the mess cowering in a far corner. It would be a while before they organized as a whole, and unless they had planned in advance, there would be confusion over their strategies and demands. The longer the situation lasted, and the better the inmates organized, the more dangerous the situation became for the Captain and his fellow hostages. If the hostage team attacked within a half-hour, the hostages' chances of survival increased dramatically. This was where the game of politics and responsibility came into play. Thorson would want to strike fast, to minimize casual-

ties. But the warden wasn't good at decisions, and she knew that, if everything went to crap, she, not Thorson, would take the blame. Unless someone higher up told her what to do, she would most likely wait it out. The hostages' best chance of survival, then, would come through negotiations. The Captain knew that he and the others, as pawns of the inmates, would likely be threatened and beaten, possibly raped and killed.

Q-Ball brushed past him and, to the Captain's surprise, left the office.

"What's happening?" Hennricks asked, wide-eyed.

"I'll let you know when I figure it out," the Captain said.

* * *

12:35pm

THE CAPTAIN HAD ENTERED THE day's activities on the shift report — and checked with Control to verify the count — when the phone rang.

"Captain, could you come into my office?" Thorson said.

Not again, he thought. "I'll be right over," he said. He slid his chair back, took a swig from a fresh diet Coke, straightened his tie, and took a few steps toward the door before realizing he had left his glasses on the desk. As he reached for them, he saw Joshua Edwards's face card and grabbed that too. Something told him that Edwards's upset over a homosexual inmate in Sgt. Alvarez's unit would be Thorson's topic, no matter that Edwards had dropped his resistance and gone quietly when faced with reason.

"I hear you had a little trouble in Nine today," Thorson said, as the Captain eased in the door, closing it behind him.

Thorson's minion, O'Malley, was in her place in the chair next to the desk, pen and pad at the ready.

"I answered a Code One." He handed Thorson the face card. "This guy went after the sergeant. When I got there, he was working himself up to a brawl. He told me he wasn't going to go to the hole, and that I'd have to fight him. I told him that wasn't going to happen."

"Did you try to cuff him?" Thorson bounced a pencil, erase end down, off his desk, with a "tap-tap-tap" of Chinese drip torture.

"Nope." The Captain stood with his arms crossed; he hadn't been invited to sit. "The way he moved back, and as upset as he was, I knew if I put hands on him, the fight was on." The Captain paused, knowing he was about to sound like a broken record. He inwardly sighed. "I didn't want to risk getting him, my staff or myself hurt."

"Is that why you called for chemicals and the Taser?"

"Basically, it was a bluff. I knew he didn't want to fight. If he did, he would have come at me. But he couldn't back down without good reason because the inmates in the rec' yard were watching through the dayroom window. When I put out the call for chemicals and the Taser and additional staff, it allowed him to save face and back down without a fight. When he gets back to the unit, he can tell his friends, "I was gonna kick their ass, but Man, there was too many Police and there ain't no way I was gonna let 'em juice me."

The Security Director shook his head, then looked at the inmate's face card. "What if he called your bluff and fought?"

"Then I'd have gassed him and hit him with the Taser. The guy is in for aggravated assault of a police officer and attempted murder. Plus, he's six-foot, six inches and three-hundred-seventy-five pounds. I'm getting too old to be rolling around on the floor, getting my butt kicked."

"Well, I guess you're lucky it worked," Thorson said, and O'Malley opened the door, ending the interview.

Back at his desk, the Captain worked to put it out of his mind. It was just another way for Thorson to let him know that he was watching. But the Captain was too impatient for more paperwork. He needed Wilkins — and some useful patrol work — to lift his mood. "Oak 18 to Oak 62," he said into his radio "10-25 the Admin. Building for staff transportation."

CHAPTER XI

Something was happening outside of the office. Q-Ball had left with an obvious sense of urgency. It had been almost a half-hour since the whole mess had started, and it felt to the Captain like the calm before the storm. A phone rang at the sergeant's station, across the hall from the social workers office. Leon had taken over the station because it afforded him visibility over the unit. Leon Nelson answered it and from across the hall, the Captain could hear him talking. He knew the negotiators were on the line and things were moving according to the Emergency Preparedness Plan.

The Captain hoped it was Dave Wilkins on the other end of the line. He was the best negotiator at North Woods. He could make a tele-marketer hang up on him out of sheer frustration. He couldn't hear either side of the conversation, but through the glass and bars in the door, he could see that Leon looked upset. Leon had taken the Captain's duty belt, and wore it slung over his shoulder, and across his chest, like a bandit with a bandolier of bullets. The Captain's badge still hung on the belt and Leon wore it with an air of effected authority. He spoke, listened, spoke, rubbing a hand on his scarred cheek, wincing as though in pain whenever his hand touched his cheek. Though the words were indistinguishable, by his tone, The Captain could tell that Leon was at high pitch, speaking in a loud, rapid, angry tone. It was the negotiators job to bring emotions down. The Captain knew that Wilkins — or who-ever — was trying to get a handle on what was happening, find out if anyone was hurt, figure out who was in charge and how many were involved. He was trying to end the whole thing. It could take minutes, hours, or even days.

Leon dropped the phone as an inmate yelled: "Man, there's about a hundred PO-lice comin' down the road! They's got shotguns and all kinda shit! "

"Stay away from the windows!" someone hollered. "They'll shoot yer ass."

It was weird, to the Captain, to watch a plan they'd all practiced countless times unfold, as he sat helplessly cuffed. It was scripted meticulously, down to the interruption of the negotiator's call. They were putting enough pressure on the inmates to show they meant business, to show they still had power. The Captain could imagine what the inmates in the yard were seeing: The North Woods SWAT team marching toward the unit, perfectly in step, each member thumping a thirty-inch nylon baton into this left hand as his right foot hit the ground. In their black combat uniforms, black helmets, and gloved hands, they resembled shock troops. Behind the first row, officers armed with gas guns, shotguns, and assault rifles wore black face masks and face shields that attached to their helmets, gas masks hanging in pouches at their side. The Captain had trained the SWAT officers for precisely such a moment as this. He knew that, as the inmates watched the SWAT show marching up the road, the snipers and hostage rescue team were slipping, unnoticed, into their positions.

The aim of the two-pronged attack — negotiations and a show of force — was confusion. It was working. Leon grabbed up the phone. "What the fuck you doin'?" he screamed, loud enough to be heard in the office. "You all's gonna get someone killed! You better tell them mother fuckers to back-off! What the fuck you mean, aint no one gonna get hurt? We gonna be hurtin' some of these bitches, lessen you get those mother fuckers to back-off!"

The Captain could picture the response: The SWAT team halting its advance, the negotiator crooning, "OK, I got them to stop. Now you gotta work with me." Like a chess player advancing on the King,

Wilkins — probably Wilkins — would slowly bluff Leon into believing that he was winning. He would bluff until it was time for checkmate.

"Yeah, they stopped," Leon shouted into the phone. "You jest make sure they stay stopped. Q-Ball," he yelled, "you watch them mother fuckers outside, and if they tries any hinkey shit, you let me know!"

*   *   *

12:47pm

WILKINS PULLED THE VAN UP outside of the Captain's office. "I'll be out back in the units," the Captain told Lt. Gaines, who was trying to look busy on the computer, "in case anyone misses me." He grabbed his radio and a coke and walked to the van Wilkins had waiting outside of the door. He clipped the radio to his belt and secured the shoulder mic to his epaulet on his shirt. It had gotten warm enough so he could leave his coat in the office. He opened the door and nodded a greeting to Wilkins, then he stooped to get in the van. He banged the top of his head against the door jam, as he climbed into the van. "I could feel that over here," Wilkins said.

"After hittin' my head for forty six years, you'd think I'd learn to duck."

"They didn't teach you that at white-shirt school? How to duck?"

"Naw, they just taught us how to persecute you poor, unfortunate blue-shirts."

"I hear that," Wilkins chuckled. "Dough-head must have been at the head of the class." Dough-head — Capt. Roland Hafbeck— was despised by the line staff, and he wasn't much trusted by his fellow white-shirts. He was a head hunter

He preformed all internal investigations against staff, and did so with zeal. He had cost more than one officer undeserved time off, yet, through his incompetence as an investigator, just as many that were guilty had been allowed to skate free. He was a legend in his own mind. Yet, because he had gone to High School with Thorson and they were hunting buddies, he was virtually untouchable. Dough-head tried to insinuate himself into any type of investigation that was being conducted. On many occasions, he had claimed credit for the work of others. Those who didn't call him Dough-head called him "Clouseau," after the inept inspector in the "Pink Panther." He was also the head of the SWAT team, and though he was otherwise considered and asshat, he was good at that part of his job.

"You better watch it, Dave," the Captain said. "Dough-head and I are pretty tight. I might put him on your case for being insubordinate!"

"Could you, please?" Wilkins pleaded. "The last guy he investigated was off for two months on pay status, and came back with "all allegations unfounded." I could use a couple of months off with pay."

"That's all you need. Two months on a bar stool! There'd be some happy liquor distributors in town!"

"Are you sayin' I'm a drunk?" Wilkins glanced over at the Captain, puffing out his chest indignantly.

"I don't know. What do you think? Are you a drunk?" The Captain looked hard at him.

"Well, if I am, I'm a functional drunk!"

"Seriously, Dave, you should lighten up on the booze a little."

"It ain't that bad." The car radio droned in the background as they cruised. Every now and then, a call went out on the State radio and they paused to listen for their call numbers. They each had assigned numbers, and the car they were in, though numbered itself, was numbered only for identification from the towers.

"Oh, come on!" the Captain said. "You take off every Friday so you can hang one on — after softball in the summer or bowling in the winter. When you do come to work on a Friday, you're like death warmed over! What do you do on your days off?"

"I don't drink much on my days off!"

"That's because your wife is there to watch you! Remember what happened when she went to California for two weeks with her parents?"

"Yeah, I guess I did put a few too many down."

"A few too many? You got gout and needed a liver scan!"

"I got the gout from too much rich food."

"Pickled eggs and pretzels aren't that rich!"

"Yeah, well, just because you beat your wife when you get drunk is no reason for me to stop!" Dave smiled, but there were teeth in what he said. The Captain had grown up as the child of a drunk and had chosen, ultimately, not to follow in those footsteps. As a youth, he had not been a "happy drunk," and in the early days of his marriage, he had come close to striking his wife in a drunken fit of anger. They were fighting over some inconsequential thing; neither of them could even remember. Maura, being a hot-blooded Romanian, was never cowed by his bluster. He'd lashed out a closed fist at her, changing the direction of the blow in the last milli-second and punching a hole in the wall. For the first time in their marriage, Maura was frightened by him, and he was horrified and filled with shame. He'd vowed never to get drunk again, and he'd quit drinking altogether when LeAnn was born. He didn't hesitate to go to parties; he just didn't drink. He didn't miss it.

His only mistake, he supposed, was telling Wilkins about the wall-punching incident. He'd only meant to empathize; Wilkins's father, like his, had been an alcoholic. But Wilkins couldn't resist gossiping that "the Captain doesn't drink because he beats his wife when he's drunk." Gossip was one of the engines that kept Wilkins running.

The Captain gave it one last try. "You know what can happen when booze takes over, Dave. I just want you to be careful. You're too good a man to end up in a bottle, and now that you're gonna be a daddy, you have to start thinking about it. There's a lot more to life than the bottle, and there's no time to waste. It seems like I only started working and raising a family yesterday. In a little over five years, I'll have my 30 in, my youngest will be out of high school, and my oldest will be done with college - or she'd better be!"

"How'd you ever end up working in the system?" Wilkins asked, changing the subject.

Though he was wise to the change the Captain took the bait. "I was waiting to be hired in Willington as a cop; I'd just finished with Criminal Justice classes and gotten married, and I was working in a door factory. But I'd applied at the state, too; I'd taken the test for Corrections and I scored high enough that I got an interview and they offered me a job." He looked out the window. An inmate yard crew was raking leaves by the school complex. A couple of inmates looked up and waved. The Captain waved back.

"The job at the factory paid more, but I was going nuts! I worked next to a fifty-nine-year-old woman who had been doing the same job for forty years. We operated a wood-jointer machine. She pushed the pieces in one side of the machine, and when they came out, I turned them over to joint the other side. We never talked. All she did, all day long, was stand there, feeding the machine and grinning. Not a word. After two months, I'd had it. I took the state job."

"So, how come you stayed with the State? Didn't you ever get an offer as a cop?"

"I started on the prison units, and really liked what I was doing. I used to be shy, believe it or not, and the prison was a challenge. But I found out I liked working with people. The list for the police department expired, and I never reapplied. I took the test for State Trooper a few years back and got hired, but they wanted to transfer me way up north. Maura was pregnant with our second kid at the time, and it just wasn't a good time to move. Later I was offered a full time patrol job for the city, but the pay and benefits just weren't there. So, here I am!

"So how'd you start working part-time as a cop?" Wilkins asked.

"I guess I started questioning whether I'd made the right choice. When I turned forty, I was offered the opportunity to attend the State Police Academy, and I got the job for the Village."

"So which do you like better? Did ya make the right choice?"

"Yeah, I think I did. I like working as a cop, but it can get pretty boring. There's nights where I've had only one or two stops and no radio calls. Then, there's been nights where I can't finish the paperwork from one stop or call before I get another one. You never know what it's gonna be."

There were times, in truth, when the Captain regretted his decision to stick with the prisons, but he was old enough to realize that at times, he would have regretted any decision. "I was working patrol last night," he said, "and I pulled over an ex-con."

"Who was it?"

"Remember a biker named Hauptmann?"

"Not off the top of my head."

"He did five or six years. He was kind of a tough bastard, but never a real problem child. He got out a few years back. Anyways, I was running radar and snagged a car speeding. When I got to the driver's door, I thought I recognized him. I asked for his license and told him I had him going seventy in a fifty-five. I don't think he could see my face. He gave me the usual. 'I know I was speeding a little, but I didn't think I was going that fast.' I had to lean over to get his license, and I think he saw me then and the light started to go on. I went back and ran his information on the computer, and I could see him looking at me in the outside mirror. He came back clean, so I just wrote him up for speeding. When I went back up to his car, he said, 'Hey Cap! I thought I recognized you! What you doin' out here?' He said he's been clean for four years. He works at a feed mill over in New Berlin. He's divorced, but he has shared custody of a three-year-old son. I think he's doing OK."

"How'd he react when you gave him the ticket?"

"He owned up, 'I kinda expected that. I know I was doin' at least 70.' Then he wanted to talk like it was old home week! He asked about Tiny, the big bald guy, all tatted up from top to bottom. I told him that the last I knew, Tiny was in Superman. Then he asked about 'Mad Dog' summers!"

Wilkins laughed. Dewey summers — Mad Dog — was an officer who looked like the actor, Wally Cox, all of five foot, six inches tall and weighing one fifty, dripping wet. He wore thick horn rimmed glasses and never raised his voice. Yet, to the inmates, he was Mad Dog because he was the most patient man ever to search a cellblock. He could find anything: a pin-joint, a shank made out of a toothbrush, extra canteen, an odd pill........anything. If it was in their cell and shouldn't be, Dewey found it. He'd retired four years ago, and the last anyone heard, he was on an archeological dig somewhere in the New Mexico desert.

"Hauptmann thought it made perfect sense," the Captain said. "He said, 'Man, he was always catching me with something! You know as well as I do, if there's anything to find in that desert, Mad Dog will find it!'"

"I'm glad you saw Hauptmann," Wilkins said. "It makes me feel good to see someone change his life and do something with himself. It reminds me that even with the revolving door, there are a lot of people we never see again. I guess there's hope for all of us!"

"You got that right," the Captain said. "In prison, guys are always planning and scheming and trying to get away with something — and sometimes the inmates are just as bad!"

"There you go again!" Wilkins said, throwing him a dubious glance. "Two thousand comedians out of work, and I have to sit and listen to you!"

"You should consider yourself lucky! With all the stuff you've pulled, you've never gotten in any real trouble!"

"What are you talking about?" Wilkins frowned.

The Captain leaned toward him. "You really want to know? 'Cause if you really want to know, I'll tell you."

"Yeah," Wilkins said, indignantly. "I'd really like to know!"

"Well, a couple of weeks ago when you took overtime in the gatehouse, I heard a little story about you, Sgt. Lenz, and a camera. Bring anything to mind?"

Wilkins looked out his window, playing innocent. "I don't know what you're talking about," he said.

"Let me refresh your memory. It was a cold, rainy day. About nine o'clock, a middle aged couple pulled in driving a brand new Cadillac sedan. Sound familiar?"

Wilkins was staring out the window, as though the passing wall of the school complex was way more interesting than the Captain's story.

"Anyways, they brought a camera into the gatehouse with them. When they were told they couldn't bring it into the prison, the gentleman got very indignant! How dare you tell him that he couldn't take the camera in to take a picture of his poor, innocent son! How dare you suggest that he walk all of the way to his car, in the pouring rain, to put the camera away! The very nerve of you, a 'civil servant,' telling him what to do."

Wilkins avoided eye contact; his ears were turning red.

"'I'll just leave my camera here,' says the gentleman. 'The least you can do is watch it!'"

"OK, OK," Wilkins said. "He put the camera on the counter and told me to watch it. I told him he could either take it to his car or put it on the coat rack, but either way, I wasn't responsible for it. It was still there when he left three hours later. He said he was surprised that it hadn't disappeared."

"Well then, just think how surprised he was when he had the film developed! Now, I'm not sayin' who, but someone told me that a couple of fine, professional officers took the camera, went into the back room of the gatehouse, and took extreme close-up shots of each other mooning the camera! I heard the shots were good enough to be published in a proctologist's textbook."

Wilkins's face was a deep, burning red.

"And," the Captain continued, "Someone told me these fine, young officers took off all their rings and watches and took the pictures against a plain wall, so they couldn't be identified. What do you think about that?"

"Well," Wilkins stammered, "I think they were probably using good, criminal thinking!"

The Captain suppressed a smile. "Seriously, Dave, if that guy sends the pictures to the Warden and Dough-head starts to investigate, you'll end up with at least thirty days suspension. They might even fire you."

"Man, as soon as we did it, I knew it was stupid! How'd you find out?"

"The son talked to me. When they got the pictures, his stepmother almost killed the old man! It seems he has a "history," and she thought he took the pictures. The son can't stand the old man. He laughed like crazy when he told me about it. He's figured out what happened, but he isn't going to tell his parents. You really dodged a bullet on this one."

Wilkins nodded his head slowly. He put a hand to his heart, grateful. The radio blared. "Attention all responders: Code Two fire alarm, Unit Ten. Code Two fire alarm, Unit Ten. Responders acknowledge!"

"Probably some ignorant inmate smoking too close to the smoke alarm, again," the Captain said, after Wilkins responded.

"I don't think I've ever been to a live fire alarm," Wilkins said, wheeling the van around to head back toward the unit. "How about you?"

"Once. Just once." The Captain didn't explain.

Wilkins stepped on the gas; the Captain watched the intersections. It took thirty seconds to reach the Unit Ten, where Sgt. Murphy was already herding inmates out the back door. "Move it Guys," he yelled, "I ain't gonna spend a month writing reports if one of you gets barbequed!"

The alarm was piercing; the Captain covered his ears as they went in. "No smoke," he said to no one in particular. The fire alarm indicator panel showed the alarm was from cell twenty-seven. Wilkins went there, while the Captain and Sgt. Murphy made sure nobody was left in the unit.

"Nothing in twenty-seven" Wilkins yelled.

"The dayroom is clear," Murphy said.

"Halls clear," announced the Captain, "looks like a false alarm."

Murphy counted the inmates in the outside recreation area and compared his count to the "out-count" board. "They're all accounted for!" he yelled over the wail of the alarm. He sent over and silenced it, then called the inmates back into the unit.

"False fire alarm, Unit Ten. Unit Ten is secure," the Captain radioed to Control.

"10-4, Oak 18," Control replied. "All Oak units, Unit Ten, false alarm. Unit Ten is secure."

"Murph, bring 'em back in," the Captain ordered.

"OK, guys," Murphy yelled, "take it in." Like a herd of cattle, the grumbling inmates lumbered back into the unit.

"Who's in twenty-seven?" the Captain asked.

Without looking at the roster, Murphy said: "That would be Winters and LaFlore. I'll get them for you." He went down the hall and returned with two inmates.

"OK," said the Captain, "which one of you set off the alarm?"

Neither answered. Antonio Winters was a wanna-be Rastafarian with grimy, matted dreadlocks halfway down his round, black face. He wore his pants low, though it was hard to tell if he was being stylish or just because he was fat. His green state issued T-shirt hung loosely around his thick belly. Hosey LaFlore was the opposite" his head was clean-shaven, his pants creased to a razors edge and his shirt buttoned to the top collar around his pencil thin neck. Their silence continued, with each avoiding the Captain's probing eyes.

"Look," the Captain finally said after 10 seconds of silence, "we can do this two ways. The first is for you to play 'big-time convict' and keep quiet, and the second is to be a man and admit responsibility. Now, if you want to do it the first way, I'll put both of you in Seg' for the next three weeks, while I conduct a full investigation. Then you'll get conduct reports and spend the next three or four months in lock-up. Or, one of you admits to it, I let Sgt. Murphy take care of business, and nothing goes on paper. So, what's it going to be?"

The inmates looked at each other for a few more seconds. Finally Winters spoke up. "Cap'n, I was layin' on the upper bunk when Frenchy passed me a butt. I guess I wasn't thinkin', and I blew some smoke toward the ceilin'. It musta set off the alarm."

"I assume you're Frenchy?" the Captain asked LaFlore. He nodded. The Captain turned to Murphy. "Sarge, can you think of an appropriate punishment for these two desperadoes?" As he said this, each inmate's eyes widened.

"I'm sure I'll come up with something. You two can wait in your cell while I think about it."

Both inmates exhaled, sounding like a balloon going flat. "C'mon, Cap'n! Don't let Murph take care of biddness! Why don'cha jus' put us in da hole for a couple of days! You don't know what Murph is gonna have us do!" Frenchy whined. "Las' time, he had us scrubbin' the outside walls with a pail of soapy water and a brush! An' it was ony about twenty degrees outside! Can't you jes give us a ticket and handle it from there?" It appeared that they feared the wrath of Murphy more than they did segregation time!

"I can do that, if you want. But it'll go on your record, and when the program board looks at it, they won't give you minimum classification. If it's handled in the house, they're none the wiser. Which do you want?"

"We'll take whatever Murph thinks up," Winters said quickly, though with great reservation. Frenchy nodded, dejectedly, and they walked away, looking at their feet and shuffling away as though they were on their way to the gallows. Heaven only knew what Murph would think up for them. Sometimes it was better if the Captain didn't know.

"So, how's life treating you?" the Captain asked Murphy.

"Shitty, Sir!"

"As I thought."

"How about some coffee?" Murphy asked.

"Not today. I've already had a couple of cups, and I'm afraid it'll stunt my growth."

"It's a little late for that." Murphy said, looking up at the Captain. "Maybe you should have started drinking it when you were ten."

"I did," said the Captain. "Just think what would have happened if I didn't! You hear anything from Abe?"

Abbas Hamdan Mahmoud, or Abe, as he was known, was a retired corrections officer. He was all of five foot eight and one hundred seventy pounds, yet with his pencil thin mustache and crisp military bearing, he'd been a source of fear for many inmates. They all thought he knew some type of ancient killing arts and could hurt them in an instance if he chose to do so. The truth would have terrified them. He had been an Officer in Sadaam Hussiens Republican Guard and was in charge of a killing team that would slip into towns and villages at night and silently kill, with their hands and perhaps a garrote, with the purpose to turn fear into terror. He had defected from Iraq in 1991, during the Gulf Invasion when he realized what his country had become, and more so, what he had become. The promise of freedom and a shortcut to American citizenship were also part of the bait. He fled, taking his two youngest children, a son and a daughter with him to freedom in the United States. He had planned to send for his wife and his two older sons as soon as he was settled in, but by then it was too late, and for twenty years, he'd heard nothing of them. He feared, but was never able to confirm that they had been killed by the very men he had once commanded. He took the job in corrections in 1995, and after twenty years, he retired, never having remarried.

"I got a letter from him about two weeks ago," Murphy said. "He was staying with in Texas with his daughter, a school teacher, and his mother came over to visit from Basra. She's ninety-two, and she told him his oldest son had survived and was a school teacher too. He asked me to send him a bunch of school supplies, pencils, paper, writing tablets and stuff for his son's school."

"What about his wife and other son?" said Wilkins.

"They were rounded-up and killed. He didn't go into much detail except to say they had been killed and that he couldn't think of the torture they had to endure."

"Man, I'll bet he feels some big-time guilt over that!" Wilkins exclaimed, "I know I would, just up and leaving like that."

"It's not like he had a lot of choice. He was about an hour ahead of the execution team that was hunting him down when he got out of the country. He did what he could."

"Still, however we justify it, I'm sure he thinks it's his fault." Wilkins said.

Not many people other than Murph, Abe and the Captain knew the story of Murph and Abe. In 1990, Murph was a Sgt. in Iraq, a Ranger with a forward intelligence team that often ventured behind enemy lines. His job was the mirror image of his adversary, Col. Mahmoud. During one such mission, Murph had arranged a meeting with Col. Mahmoud.....Abe — who he discovered wanted to defect. They had to make it look like he had been taken prisoner so his family wouldn't be in danger. Sgt. Murph and his team knew where Abe was housed and crept to his villa, leaving behind men as rear cover guards. Entering the stone house, Murph and his partner spotted a lone guard, a toughened Republican Guard regular. Murph slid behind the man, clapped a hand over his mouth with his left hand, and slit his throat with the blade in his right. Abe jumped from his bed and engaged his engaged "captors" in mock struggle, before allowing them to cover his head and drag him from the tent. As it turned out, the lone witness to the hooded colonel being dragged away was an elderly woman. She was too scared to sound any alarm, but she confirmed the abduction.

Because Abe trusted Murph, they became confidants, allies and friends. While Abe supplied information that saved countless numbers of American lives, the ruse was discovered and he was considered a traitor to his own country. In a hastily conceived plan he was able to leave for the United States with only two of his children, with the promise his wife and other children would soon follow. The Republican Guard got to them before they could be safely secreted out of the country, and exacted their rage and vengeance about Abe, against them.

Unknown to Abe, Murph not only found Abe a place to live in the States, he also helped him find a job. Abe, in turn, helped Murphy bury the ghosts of the men he'd killed and reaffirm his faith in his own worth.

"He's doing great," Murphy said, "but I miss the hell out of the little shit."

Voices rose in the dayroom; two inmates were arguing. With an audible sigh, Murphy leaned out the office window. "Rodriguez, Majors!" he yelled, "Get your butts out of *my* dayroom!" The two looked at each other, and without a word, went their separate ways. "Those two are having a long spat," Murphy said. "I moved them down opposite hallways, but every time they see each other, they start bickering. Man, what did I ever do to deserve two queens?"

Majors and Rodriguez were transsexuals. Each was halfway through the transformation from male to female, and though they had been roommates, they'd had no interest in each other, sexually. The pairing-up had been a happy one, until Majors accused Rodriguez of being a whore, and Rodriguez implied Majors was too ugly to be one. Before they could scratch each other's eyes out, Sgt. Murphy had separated them.

Majors had been in prison for twenty-three years for murdering a homosexual lover. The affair had gone bad when Majors had decided he was a woman locked in a man's body; he had gotten breast implants and started hormone therapy to stop the growth of his beard. Majors' lover had objected to the transformation, and in an argument, Majors had stabbed him. Of course, once Majors was in prison, the hormone therapy stopped and the testosterone kicked in, re-igniting his beard.

To solve that problem, Majors took a broken piece of a glass ashtray, and in the solitude of his cell, castrated himself. When officers entered his cell to help him, Majors hurriedly flushed his severed testicles down the toilet. He was rushed to the hospital and, minus his testicles, was soon back in prison.

He took the name Cassandra Anne, and used red ink as lipstick and black magic marker as eyeliner. With shoulder length blond hair and breasts the size of volleyballs, the 50-year-old Majors was easy to mistake for a woman — from certain angles.

A full view of his face always shattered the ruse. He had been a semi-professional boxer, and his nose was crooked nose from countless breaks. The rest of his facial features resembled a garish, drag caricature of Milton Berle.

His old roommate, William Rodriguez, was known simply as "Billie." He had been part way through the transformation when arrested for violating parole. He had been working as a prostitute and had the misfortune to offer his services to an undercover cop. From the waist up, the thirty-year-old Billie looked like an attractive Hispanic woman, with flowing black hair and large breasts.

"You know, Murph," the Captain said, "We try to match inmates with staff who will be particularly sensitive to their needs. For some reason, you were the one who came to mind for Billie and Cassandra!"

"Ain't that some shit!" Murphy said, smiling and shaking his head. "I guess I can put up with them, as long as they don't start giving me fashion tips!"

"If I see you wearing pink socks and eye liner, I'm gonna start wondering!" the Captain said.

"Just don't send me anymore! If you do, I'm gonna have to protest!" At least once a year, Murphy staged a personal "protest." No one knew when it was coming or why. On a usual day, Murphy was the picture of a professional officer: cleanly shaved, his hair combed sharply from a part on the side, his uniform sharply pressed, his collar brass gleaming, and his shoes spit shined. When a "protest" started, all that changed. He'd show up at the gatehouse in a wrinkled uniform, scruffy work boots, and his hair standing up as though he'd just rolled out of bed. He would let his salt-and-pepper beard go untrimmed and, as a whole, take on the look of a wino. Murphy had lost his two middle front teeth in a fight in the Marines, and when he was "protesting," he would leave his partial plate out, exposing a gap that would make any "Billy-Bob" jealous.

"What's the protest about?" the Captain asked once, as Murphy slouched through the gatehouse at the start of their shift.

"I'm protesting the continual harassment by management!"

"All right, Murph," the Captain asked, "what's got your goat this time?"

"Thorson told me I have to take the pigs out of my office." Murphy's pig collection included a pig coffee cup, a pig calendar, a pig notebook, and a stuffed pig wearing a State uniform. "I've had 'em in here for ten years and no one has ever complained," he said. "Now Thorson comes along and tells me I have to have them out of my office by Friday, or he'll have them taken out."

"Did he say why?"

"Nope. He just said he doesn't like 'em, and they better be gone by Friday."

"He must have said more than that."

"Oh, he started on about some crap — that they were 'unprofessional looking' and demeaning to our job. I told him if 'pig' was the worst I was called, I considered it a good day. He got all puffed up and laid down the law: 'Gone by Friday!'"

Murphy's grandson had given him the stuffed pig, and his wife and daughters had given him the rest of the knick-knacks for Christmas, birthdays, or whatever. Inmates in his unit even brought him pig pictures out of newspapers and magazines; he'd display them in his office window, as a parent would display the drawings of a child on the refrigerator.

Usually when Murphy "protested," it was more out of boredom than anything — about minor unfairness or even a politician making a stupid remark to the press about corrections officers — but this one really seemed to the Captain like real harassment. "So how long are you gonna protest?" the Captain asked.

"I don't know. My beard's just starting to look scruffy, and by next week my hair will be pretty bad. I gotta clean up after the dog, so who knows what'll be on my boots when I come in. I'll wait a few days, and then go see Thorson."

Nothing that Murphy was doing was prohibited. It was simply "frowned upon" by the administration. It galled the Captain that Thorson was making an issue of the pigs. It didn't seem to matter to Thorson that Murphy ran the cleanest, most orderly unit in the institution. It didn't seem to matter to Thorson that there were fewer disciplinary problems in Murphy's unit than in any other. It didn't seem to matter to Thorson that there was less inmate conflict or that the inmates and staff got along and respected each other. What mattered to Thorson was that he was "the boss." The Captain knew the "protest" would end as quickly as it had begun, but he had to inform Murphy officially that his uniform and appearance was substandard. Sure enough, Murph showed up at work that Friday clean shaven, in a pressed uniform, with his hair combed and shoes shined. Without a word to the inmates or anyone, he packed up the pigs and took them home.

"Wilkins," the Captain said, "I'm gonna walk to Unit Eleven. Pick me up in about ten minutes."

"Sure thing, Cap You sure you don't want to make it twenty, so I'll have a little free time?"

CHAPTER XII

"Man, I wish I wouldn't have answered the phone and taken this shit job for overtime today," Phil Adams said, tears filling his eyes. The Captain had known Adams for twenty years. His regular job was as Segregation officer, but when a unit officer had called in sick, Adams had stepped up. He was newly married, for the second time, and had just moved into a house two blocks away from the Captain's. His wife was a social worker at the prison, and there was no doubt that she knew her husband was a hostage.

"They're starting to bring the troops in," The Captain said. ""They won't do anything yet. They don't know where we are in the building, and they'll try to negotiate until they find out. Wilkins will be talking with the inmates and you know him as well as I do: He'll get what he needs. But if the inmates try to do something stupid, the shit will hit the fan. We may get gassed along with the inmates, so don't let that scare you. Hit the ground and try to get under cover until you're told to come out. Capt. Halfbeck will bring the troops in. No matter what you think of him, he's good at that job and so are the guys with him." His guys would no doubt include Murphy, Warinski, Dern, Zielke and Sgt. Bergman.

Thinking about it, the Captain knew that Thorson, for all of his bluster, probably had good instincts in an emergency. The big question, in the Captain's mind, was whether or not Thorson would fall victim to pressure from above.

161

Q-Ball burst back into the room, his face full of rage, spittle fly-ing like mist from his mouth. "Man, you PO-lice is fuckin' with the wrong peoples! "

"What's happening?" the Captain asked.

Q-Ball shook his head. "Youse is fuckin' with the wrong peoples." His fists clenched and unclenched nervously at his side. He appeared to be working himself up to something he felt needed to be done.

"Q-Ball," the Captain said, "no one in here is trying to fuck with you. We're just trying to figure out what's happening."

Q-Ball brought his face close to the Captain's. His sweat smelled of fear. "What's happenin' is that they's all kinds of PO-lice out front wif all kinds of guns. We gots a man on the phone tellin' us he don't wanna see nobody hurt. He be tellin' us that he tryin' to help us, to keep calm! He be sayin' all kinds of shit, but he aint doin' nuffin'!" Q-Ball grabbed the front of the Captain's shirt, pulling him closer. "They gots all kinds of guns and shit out there, and they be tellin' us to come out with our hands up. Fuck that! We aint givin' up! We gon' be gettin' what we want! We be axin' for stuff an he don't be givin' us nuffin'. Leon say that if'n we don' get somethin' soon, he gonna hafta hurt someone." He pushed the Captain away and walked rapidly to the door, peering through the window from an angle.

Taking a deep breath, the Captain said, "Q-Ball, so far you've been real good to us. I'll remember that. I hope you don't let anything happen to any of us."

"Shit, " Q-Ball said, turning toward the Captain, "I ony been good cause Leon tol' me to be. I can be real bad, if'n Leon tells me to be bad. If'n Leon tells me to cut yer fuckin' head off, it's as good as gone, motherfucker!" He turned back to his spot by the window.

The Captain didn't doubt it. He could Captain Halfbeck trying to talk to the inmates on a bullhorn, exhorting them to give up before things got worse.

"Fuck da Po-lice!" someone called, and several inmates took it up as a chant.

The Captain knew that the assault teams would be moving into positions for an assault. They would strike all of the doors at the same time, with the exception of one. They would leave open the door that the inmates had most heavily barricaded. The inmates could run out that door — through the mess they had made and the traps they had set — into the hands of a waiting SWAT Team. They had trapped themselves in a killing box, and though they had yet to realize it, it was only a matter of time.

*   *   *

1:15PM

IT WASN'T A VERY LONG walk to Unit Eleven. The Captain was taking his time, enjoying what nature had to offer. He walked leisurely, the afternoon sun slanting through clouds, and the autumn leaves making the landscape a jig-saw puzzle of colors. The smell of fall was sharp, and the Captain reveled in it. About one hundred yards away, on the other side of the perimeter fence, he spotted five White-tailed deer walking on the perimeter road. He watched until they left the road and disappeared into the forest. The Tower officers often threw bread from their meal trays, and while the deer were wary of humans, some would venture close to look for offerings. In another month, when hunting season opened, many of them would bed down near the base of the towers. Hunters were restricted from coming near the prison grounds, and the deer knew it. "Strange," thought the Captain, "the same towers that protect me from people protect the deer from people."

Inmates passed him along the right side of the road, coming or going from classes. Some turned away or faced the ground, while others brightened.

"How ya' doin', Cap?"

"What's up, Cap?"

""Doin' good. How about you, Wilson, stayin' out of trouble?

"Man, Cap, you know how it is! Trouble just seems to find me!"

"It sure doesn't have to look too far, does it? I hardly recognized you, not wearing orange!" Inmates in segregation, Wilson's usual status, usually wore bright orange clothes. In regular status, as he was today, Wilson was wearing prison issued greens.

"Trouble just comes to me!" Wilson smiled.

"Cap, you gave me thirty days building confinement," a short, stocky man said. "Man. that's just brutal! I can't go anywhere except school! Is there any way to shorten it?"

"Sorry. You had ten days to appeal it to the Warden. If I gave you thirty days, you had it coming!"
"I ain't sayin' I didn't! But thirty days! Man, that just ain't right! All I did was get in a little argument! Why do I gots to do thirty days?"

"If it doesn't hurt, it isn't punishment. How much you got left?"

"Ten more days."

"All I can tell you is to stick it out. Don't be getting into any more trouble over it."

"I won't, Cap but thirty days! Man, that's just brutal!"

The Captain didn't remember the inmate's name or what he had done. He processed so many conduct reports each week that he rarely recalled specific infractions or specific inmates, unless he saw them time after time.

He walked up the two steps into unit eleven, taking a final deep breath of the autumn air. Looking around, he saw the hallways and dayroom were empty, with a crowd of inmates by the Sgts. desk. Sgt. Sylvia Gilson was at the desk, checking inmates out on the status board. A dozen or so were lined up, waiting to give their name, cell number, and where they were going. The Captain waited outside the office until the last man had left.

Sgt. Gilson stood, as the Captain entered. "Afternoon," she said, smiling, and sat back down, nodding at the Captain to take a seat. Sgt. Gilson was Puerto Rican, and possessed the beauty of the islanders. She was curvaceous — the inmates called that "thick" — and her dark skin and black, almond eyes made her popular among newcomers, until they realized that she had little tolerance for misbehavior and less tolerance for flirtatious behavior.

"How's life treating you?" the Captain asked. Gilson was recently divorced, with three children. Her first ex-husband had recently moved back from out of state; he had done time for beating and raping her fifteen years ago. Her second ex-husband was a wannabe musician who rarely paid child support. Gilson worked at least twenty-four hours of overtime a week to support her family.

"With some of these guys, it's like dealing with a bunch of overgrown teenagers!" Gilson said. "Long's cell mate will probably be out to talk to you."

"What's up with him?"

"He said Long is gettin' pretty nasty. I didn't ask for details, but he said he'd like to talk to you if you came in today."

"OK, I'll check with him before I go. Isn't Long the one they call 'Country?'"

"Yup, that's him."

"OK," I'll deal with him in a little bit. First, the important stuff: "Working a double, today?"

"Nope. Emily, has a volleyball game tonight, and I told her I'd come see it. I think she plays against your daughter's team, doesn't she?"

"I think so. I don't know why you're bothering to go, just to watch your daughter lose!"

"Yeah, right. I told her all she has to do is hit the ball toward Marie, and she'll get a point every time!" Marie was the same age as Sgt. Gilson's middle daughter, and they'd competed in soccer and basketball, as well as volleyball. Each was usually the best player on her team.

"Marie's been working on spiking, so watch out!"

Gilson smiled. "It's fun to watch them compete."

"How's Abe doing?" the Captain asked. Sgt. Gilson's sixteen-year-old son had been giving her trouble for a couple of years.

"I've got to go to court with him next Thursday," she said. "I hope they don't put him in juvenile detention, but I don't know what to do with him. I thought he learned his lesson last summer, when he was breaking car windows. I told the judge that it wasn't a good idea for him to live with his father, but that's what he wanted. Then he gets caught drinking. But since he's been back with me, he's doing better."

"I hope it goes OK at court, but don't be surprised if he gets a few days in 'juvey.' They'll still let him out for school every day."

"I don't know. Maybe it's what he needs. I'm at the end of my rope."

"It's got to be frustrating," the Captain said. "But look at the whole picture: I did a lot of stupid things when I was a kid, and I'm sure you made one or two mistakes yourself! We both turned out OK."

"Do you really think so?" she said, meeting the Captain's eyes. "Sometimes I think we're as locked up as the inmates." She looked out the window. "Here comes Wills. He's Long's roommate."

Wills was tall and lanky. The Captain could tell he had done time on more than one occasion. He walked with a swagger, his right arm "scooping" behind him with each step. His prison greens hung low on his hips, and the shirt was at least two sizes too big. He wore his own Nike tennis shoes, bright red, no doubt signaling his gang affiliation.

"Capn, I gots to talk wif ya about my celly. Country be puttin' dookie all over da flo! Ever' time he gets outta bed, dude don' wash up or nuffin. He takes his stinkin' ass an' jes gets in the chow line. Then, if'n he goes in the bafroom, he busts a grumpy and then he don' ever wipe his ass! Dude be smellin' like dookie! He came in dis monin'' and gots dookie running down his leg! I tol' him to clean up, and all he does is take his stinkin' ass pants and filthy underwear, and put 'em in a bag, and set it in the corner! The whole room be smellin' like shit! You gots to do somethin' or someone gonna hurt that boy! He gots the whole hall ready to blaze his ass, he so nasty!"

The Captain knew about Long and his problem. He was a small, ferret-looking white kid, a little slow, mentally. He had a hard time taking care of himself, and it was difficult finding anyone who wanted to cell with him; his reputation often preceded him. He couldn't control his bowels. The Captain had talked to health services, and they'd given Long some adult diapers, but he refused to wear them. He had been in seven different units, and each time, he had to be moved for his own safety.

"Where's your celly now?" the Captain asked.

"He be in the shower. I don' know why, though. He come out smellin' jes' as bad as when he went in! Dude don' know how to wash hisself! Then, he put on the same stanky clothes! Dude is jes plain ol' nasty!"

Through the window the Captain could see his Wills's celly leaving the shower, another inmate close behind him. The other inmate came over to the office door. "Cap, you better talk to Country. He just took a shower, and there's a big pile of crap sittin' in the corner. If he stays here, he's gonna get hurt."

They were right. Someone would hurt Country if he stayed in the unit. Last time, the Captain had called a shrink to talk to Long, and the shrink had said it was a medical problem. But Long had insisted, "I'm a man, and I aint wearin' no diapers!" He'd promised the Captain that he'd try to control himself. That was three days ago.

"Oak 18 to Oak 63 and 64. 10-25 Unit Eleven," the Captain radioed, summoning help from his patrol officers. Then he turned to Sgt. Gilson. "I'm going to place Long in seg. If I leave him in here, it's only a matter of time before someone beats him."

"I don't know if I could blame them," Gilson sighed. "I sure wouldn't want to live with him."

The Captain, Wilkins, and Walters, the other officer who'd responded, put on latex gloves and headed down the hall. As they neared Long's room, the pungent aroma of human waste filled their nostrils.

"Man, I hope he don't fight!" Wilkins said. "I hate rolling around in shit."

"It's not high on my list of fun, either," the Captain said, "but I don't think he'll give us a problem. If he does, we'll take care of business."

Long was alone in the room. The Captain rapped sharply on the door and motioned him out into the hall. "Mr. Long, do you remember what we talked about a couple of days ago?" the Captain said.

"Yeah, I remember," Long said, forlorn. The odor of shit rose off him.

"I told you then that if you couldn't control yourself, you'd be placed in Seg'. I've gotten a lot of complaints that you're messing yourself again." The Captain felt sorry for Long, who looked at his feet, ashamed.

"I've been tryin'," Long pleaded.

"I know you have. But trying isn't good enough. The nurse told me you're not using what they gave you."

"Man, I told you before, I ain't gonna wear no diapers!"

"Then I've got no choice. Mr. Long, I want you to turn around and face the wall with your hands behind your back, palms together. I can't let you stay in this unit, It's not safe for you." The two patrol officers moved to each side of Long, who reluctantly turned to face the wall. The officers cuffed him quickly.

Wilkins looked at Walters. "It looks like you get the pleasure of shaking him down. I got seniority."

'Figures," said Walter, grinning, "stick it to the black man!" He made sure his rubber gloves were pulled above his wrists and started the search, silently retching a time or two. When he'd finished, he had tears in his eyes. He and Wilkins each took hold of an arm and escorted Long out of the unit. Some of the inmates, watching from their cells, broke into applause. It was better than when the Captain took Long out of Unit Two, when the inmates had sung, " Naa-Naa- Naa-Naa, Hey-Hey, Goodbye."

"It's no wonder that this kid is screwed-up," the Captain thought. "No one has ever given a damn about him." At the Seg' building, Long was showered again, given a clean orange jumpsuit, and placed in a cell. As he left the building, the Captain could hear inmates hollering and laughing at Long. "Nothing else that happens today will make me more thankful for my life and the blessings I've been given," the Captain thought. But he was about to be proven wrong.

CHAPTER XIII

Q-Ball paced the room, clenching and unclenching his fists. He stopped, from time to time, to wipe the sweat off of his bald head. He took a sip from a cup of water on the desk. The Captain thought of the ice-cold Diet Coke he had left in the car. He thought of how easy it would be to take Q-Ball out of the picture. He knew that if he made a move, Adams and Hennrick would follow his lead. But he also knew that nothing good could come of messing with Q-Ball. There was no escape; the three of them would be trapped with the rioting inmates.

It had been quiet for a while. The SWAT Teams must have settled into position. Leon was still talking on the phone, probably to Wilkins. "Q-Ball, what's happening out there?" the Captain said. "Is everything OK?"

"Eveything is fine. We's jes figgurin out what ta do next. Don' you be worryin' about it."

The photo-identification card still hung around Q-Ball's neck, outside his crisp, white, increasingly sweat-stained T-shirt: Quincy Belmont.

"They call you 'Q-Ball' 'cause you don't like Quincy?" the Captain asked.

Q-Ball turned to face the Captain. "That's right. Never did like that name. Got me beat up a lot when I was little, so's when I got

171

bigger, I had eveyone call me 'Q.' When I shaved my head, they changed it to Q-Ball."

"Which do you like better: 'Q' or 'Q-Ball?'"

Q-Ball looked at the Captain, and a brief smile crossed his lips. "My friends call me 'Q.' Eveyone else calls me Q-Ball."

The Captain smiled. "I know what you mean about names. They can sure bring trouble. When I was a kid, I used to get all kinds of grief over my first name."

"What's yer name?" Q-Ball asked.

Before the Captain could answer, a generator roared to life outside the building and Q-Ball jumped. "Shut the fuck-up," he said. "Looks like they's tryin to pull some more shit. You best hope Leon don't get pissed over it."

Q-Ball left the office, and the Captain whispered, "Looks like they're geared up for an assault. I don't think it'll come for a while. Right now, it's just a show."

"You think they'll come in to get us?' Hennricks asked, his sparse attempt at a real mustache quivering on his upper lip.

"Not yet, " the Captain said. "As long as no one has been hurt, they'll try to negotiate. They'll wait it out. When they do come in, we'll be their first priority. They lost their first window of opportunity. The cons know that something is coming, they just don't know when. We won't either, until it happens. Sooner or later though, if negotiations break down, it WILL happen."

"So, you're telling us that one of us has to get hurt for something to get done?" Hennricks whispered loudly, fear evident in his voice "That's bullshit!"

"I hear what you're saying, and I'm not any happier about it than you are. But that's the way it is. We're all a lot safer if the negotiations succeed." To reassure him, he added, *"It'll all be over soon. I know you're scared, Son, but so are they. Hell, so am I, but all we can do is wait. I'll do what I can to make sure they don't hurt us anymore, OK?"* Hennricks leaned back in his chair, and at least, for the moment, felt almost like a child under the wing of a protective father.

The greatest danger for them, now, the Captain knew, was being injured during an assault. "If the troops come, don't try to run to our guys," he said. *"Chances are, the place will be filled with tear gas, and they might mistake you for an inmate. If that happens, you'll get shot."* Inching closer to them, the Captain asked quietly, *"Can either of you guys reach inside the back of my belt? I've got a handcuff key taped to the inside. If you can get it out, I can get my cuffs off."*

*   *   *

1:44pm

AS THE CAPTAIN AND WILKINS entered Unit Twelve, he could see Sgt. Bruce Lawsen in the dayroom, talking to a number of complaining inmates.

"Sarge, we can't get but three channels on TV in the cells in this unit," a lean, coffee-colored black inmate said, "and two of 'em spend the afternoon givin' the farm reports! When I was over in Nine, I got at least six! What's up with that?"

"I guess they just get better reception," Lawson said.

"Man," a tall Hispanic inmate said, "quit bitching or the Sarge will change the channel to PBS. We'll end up watching 'Sesame Street' and 'Mr. Rodgers,' and 'Barney!'" Get your ass back to your room, and let the rest of us decide!"

Sgt. Lawson cleared his throat, turning to the black inmate. "Let me repeat the rules. If you have a personal TV, you don't get a say in what's on the TV in the dayroom. Only the guys that don't have a TV can decide what to watch. If they can't come to a consensus, then I choose!" Sgt. Lawson, lately, was the most patient man at North Woods. He was retiring in two months. At fifty-four, he had a full head of wavy grey hair that made the Captain a little envious. He and the Captain had been the first two officers that the State had sent to the F.B.I. Hostage Negotiations School. Until recently, Lawsen had been head of the team, but he'd stepped into an advisory role, to let Wilkins learn to lead.

The black inmate balled his fists. "Listen, jes' cause your people is poor and don't be sendin' you no money, don't be gettin' mouthy with me!" He threw a glance at the Captain and, without out a word, slouched off to his cell.

"So, Gentlemen," Lawsen asked the inmates as they settled into chairs, "What'll it be?"

"How's about Channel Seven? Jerry's gonna have "Strippin' Grannies" on!"

"What about Rikki on Two? Hers is called "Dude Looks Like a Lady! You have to guess which ones are dudes and which ones are ladies!"

"All right!" Lawsen held up a hand. "You're about five seconds away from a singing purple dinosaur. Time to decide: which is it?"

"We'll take 'Dude looks Like a Lady' on Two," someone called, and nobody argued. Lawsen went into the office and punched the remote. The Captain and Wilkins followed.

"Gee, Sarge, looks like you're having a rough afternoon, full of big decisions!" The Captain chuckled.

"The TV situation is a pain! They get three channels in the cells, but the dayroom TV gets fifteen. So everyone wants to watch out here. I wish they'd give them cable and get it over with. It'd keep them out of my hair!"

"The public would love that. Cable TV in prisons! Remember the stink over the free weights? This would be worse."

About two years ago, a newly elected, tough-on-crime governor had hired a "professional" to assess the prisons and make recommendations on what to eliminate. The aim was to "make things rough for criminals." Without ever setting foot in a prison or asking advice from anyone who spent their days there, he implemented the advice of the "professional," who decided that taxpayers didn't want inmates to have television, free weights, music studies, or arts and crafts.

The public — including outside law enforcement — seemed to think that all the inmates did with free weights was pump themselves up to be intimidating. Cops wanted the weights gone so they wouldn't have to face ex-convicts who made Arnold Schwarzenegger look like a wuss. Yet prison officers knew that inmates who pumped iron were generally a lot less trouble. They were more interested in working out than causing mischief. They'd spend a couple of free hours every day lifting weights, and then go to school or work. They didn't screw up because they didn't want to lose "rec." privileges. To them, losing "rec." privileges was worse than the hole.

Now that the tough-on-crime governor had gotten rid of free weights, that leverage was gone. It was the same with music studies and arts and crafts: an inmate who spent his time studying guitar, drums, or piano, or making ceramics or painting, spent less time causing trouble. Without those programs, the "carrot" was gone, and only the more dangerous "stick" was left. The elimination of programs kept inmates on their units more, giving them more time to work up mischief for the unit officers.

"They gotta have something to do," Lawsen said. "Otherwise, they sit in the units and get on each other's nerves. I'm glad I only have until December to go!"

"I'll be following you, in a few," the Captain said. He turned to Wilkins. "How many do you have left, Dave?"

"Oh, about twenty years! You tryin' to get me depressed? One of these days, I'm gonna just walk in and quit!"

"Do that, and you'll have to work for a living," the Captain said. "That'd probably kill you!"

"Yah, you're right about that. But then again, I wouldn't have to put up with all the B.S.!"

"Put up with it?" the Captain declared. "You're usually the cause of it!"

"What are you tryin' to say?"

"I think you know just what he's sayin'!" Lawsen said.

"Who asked you, old man? Besides that, who's side are you on? I thought blue shirts stuck together? Don't let the Captain drive a wedge!"

Lawsen laughed. "You know, Dave, you not only create the B.S., you're full of it, too!"

"Not to change the subject," the Captain interrupted, "but when do you guys have negotiations training?"

"We haven't had any for about four months," Lawsen said. "With the budget crunch, there hasn't been any scheduled."

The Captain still thought of it as the "Hostage Negotiations Team," but it now had the more politically correct title, "Crisis Negotiations Team." The word, "hostage," had certain negative qualities, whereas "crisis" was perceived as less threatening. The Captain had received training as a negotiator after a riot in which fifteen staff members were taken hostage at what was then the State's only maximum security prison. He'd participated in the stand-off as part of a SWAT team. After standing outside in ten-degree weather for eleven hours, ready to battle inmates with nothing more than a wooden baton, he'd decided that if anything else came up that he could do besides freeze his butt off, he'd jump at the chance. The riot ended peacefully through negotiations, and the State decided to send a few handpicked officers from each institution for negotiations training with the FBI. The Captain had spent ten days learning the intricacies of negotiating for a person's life.

Over the years, he had put the training to good use, though it was often simply to stop inmates from hurting themselves. Once he'd stopped an inmate from hanging himself, only to read, years later, that the inmate had committed a car-jacking and in the process had shot and paralyzed a young father. He'd seen the inmate a few years later, and when the guy yelled a cheerful, "Hey Cap!" all he could think of was the paralyzed man. He'd felt a nagging sense of responsibility that had he not talked the inmate out of hanging himself, he'd have spared the young father. It took time for the Captain to realize that had he let the inmate hang himself, he'd have felt guilt for that too. He now knew that he'd done what he needed to do at the time, and it had been the right thing.

After all of his training on hostage rescue, crowd control, forcible entry, and sniper methods, hostage negotiation — or rather, crisis negotiation — was what the Captain used most, almost every day. Two days ago, he and Wilkins had been having a "normal" day when, at 1 p.m., they'd received a "Code One, Unit Fifteen, inmate with a weapon." The Captain, Wilkins and Hoover entered the unit, each from a different door. In the day-room, Officers Zielke and Dern flanked an inmate, from about ten feet away. The inmate had a hairstyle like Alfred Einstein and was at least six feet tall. His heavily muscled arms were tattoo free, and in one hand, the Captain could see that the inmate had a shank made from a toothbrush with a razor blade melted into the handle.

Sgt. Bergman called the Captain over. "Inmate Wilson just got kicked out of the sex offender program. When Dern went to tell him, he ran into the dayroom with the shank and said he'd kill anyone who tried to touch him. His first name is James."

"Call for a taser and a back-up," the Captain said quietly. "Wilkins, you're on. Do your stuff."

Wilkins approached the jittery inmate and noticed him trembling, though out of fear or rage, he couldn't tell. "James," he said. "what seems to be the problem?"

James stared at Wilkins, waving the shank. "What the fuck you care what my problems are!? You just stay back!"

The Captain stayed a few feet behind Wilkins, allowing him room to talk, ready to jump if anything happened. "James, I understand you're upset about the program, but this isn't doing anyone any good," Wilkins said. "Put the shank down."

"Stay the fuck back!" James swung the blade in front of him. "Try to grab me and I'll cut ya!"

"James, just calm down. No one is going to grab you." Wilkins signaled Dern and Zielke to back away. "Tell me what's happening."

James started to cry. "I'm sick of this shit! I'm sick of doin' time! I'm sick of life!" He drew the edge of the razor across his throat, opening a thin wound. Blood soaked the front of his T-shirt, but the Captain could see it wasn't deep.

"James!" Wilkins yelled, then, in a softer voice, "Put the shank down and let's talk about it."

"Fuck it!" James lunged forward, swinging the shank wildly at the unarmed officers. Seeing a break as they stepped back, he ran past them and up the stairs to the second tier of cells. The Captain, Wilkins and Officer Hoover ran up the stairs behind him. At the top, James was straddling the railing, ready to jump. All along the tier, inmates watched from their cell windows, up and down the range.

"James!" Wilkins yelled. "James, look at me!"

James watched the Captain, about ten feet away. "Stay back, or I'll jump!" he said. The Captain and Hoover stopped walking; their hands "bladed" in case the inmate came at them, but Wilkins continued a few steps closer.

"I'm just here to watch that nothing happens to you, James," the Captain said. "You need to talk to the officer."

"James, lets talk," Wilkins said. "Maybe we can come up with a way, together, to get this over with without anyone getting hurt."

The bleeding inmate looked at him. "It's too late for that!" He swiped the shank across his wrists, first one, then the other.

"James, don't do that," Wilkins said. "I want to help you. Let's work together on this."

"Man, what you mean, you want to help me? Don't nobody give a shit if'n I bleed to death or jump!" His leg, dangling over the top rail, kicked out in frustration.

"You're wrong, James. I care. That's why I'm here." Wilkins moved slightly closer.

"You're here because it's your job! You're here 'cause you gots to be!"

The Captain and Hoover, too, inched closer. James had moved so that he was sitting on the upper rail with his feet hooked on the outside bottom rail. The Captain figured that if he got close enough, he would have a fifty-fifty chance of grabbing James and pulling him back onto the tier.

"James, we both need to calm down," Wilkins said, his voice soothing. "I'm willing to stay here and talk with you for as long as it takes."

Below them, the Captain could see staff clearing the day-rooms and a social worker closing and locking doors, so other inmates couldn't interfere. Captain Halfbeck was coming in the door from the kitchen with a Taser. With the wave of his hand, the Captain signaled him to stay back, out of sight. James certainly didn't need any more stress.

"What you need them gloves for?" James demanded. The Captain, Wilkins and Hoover were pulling on latex gloves. Blood seeped from the superficial wounds on James' wrists. The bleeding from the larger cut across his throat had slowed to a trickle.

"I'm putting them on so I can help you," Wilkins said, as he crept closer.

"You stay back! And tell them peoples downstairs that if'n any of 'em tries comin' up, I'm jumpin'"

The Captain called out, "Stay down there! James and Wilkins are talking." He moved closer to the man on the rail. "About two more feet, he thought, "and we can grab him." As though he were reading the Captain's mind, Hoover matched him, move for move.

James stood up suddenly on the outside edge of the rail. He sobbed, "I'm nothin' but a screw-up. My whole life, I be screwin' everthing up. I just can't take it no more!" He held the rail in one hand, the shank in the other.

There was no way they could safely grab him now, the Captain knew. If they tried and missed, it would look like they'd pushed him. In his peripheral vision, he could see inmates looking out of their cells.

"James, why don't you just drop the knife, come on over here, and we'll talk," Wilkins crooned. "Dr. Wilson is on his way over, and I'll have a nurse take a look at you. I can see you're hurting." Wilkins inched closer. "There are people who care about you."

"Man," James sobbed, "the oniest peoples that ever cared about me was my Grams! And I only gets to see her twice a month!"

"James, I want you to think about this," Wilkins said. "Your Grams loves you, or she wouldn't come and see you at all. She cares about you, and so do I. I don't think you want to hurt your Grams anymore, do you?"

"I never wanted to hurt Grams!" James sobbed.

"I know that, James, and so does your Grams. Your Grams still loves you and needs you. James, come on over here, and when we're all done, you can call your Grams. She'll understand. She loves you!"

James screamed, a wail from the depths of his being over-flowing with the torment of a failed life.

The Captain was close enough to grab him, and James was distracted enough that it might work. Moving quickly, he grabbed the wrist holding the shank and shook it, gripping James' elbow in his other hand, pulling him over the rail and onto the floor as the knife clattered free. Hoover had just as quickly grabbed from the other side, and together they pulled James to safety.

"James, I'll help you," the Captain said. "Easy, guys," he told Wilkins and Hoover as they laid hands on the bleeding inmate's legs and shoulders. "James is hurt."

James cried, and Wilkins talked softly to him. "Dr. Wilson will see you in Unit Fourteen," he said. "We're going to put cuffs on you and have the nurse look at you before we go anywhere. OK?"

James nodded, and the officers helped him to his feet. Dave patted his back, reassuring him that he was all right, it was over, he was safe. Dave would deny having done it if anyone men-tioned it, but it was his gesture of humanity and compassion, to comfort a wounded soul. Wilkins was good at what he did.

In Unit Twelve, in the present, the conversation continued. "I hope you never have to use any of the fancy stuff you've learned," the Captain told Lawsen and Wilkins. Then, jokingly, he said, "Just remember: you're first priority is to save the Cap-tains ass!"

"Yeah, right!" Lawsen said. "If they grab you, I'm taking a long lunch!"

Wilkins laughed, and added, "They'd let you go just so they wouldn't have to feed you!".

"You better hope nothing g happens to me," the Captain said, "if I'm not around, who's gonna cover for your lame ass?"

"There he goes again, trying to drive a wedge!" Lawson said.

CHAPTER XIV

Phil Adams reached up with his cuffed hands and felt along the back of the Captain's inner belt. He ran his fingers along the smooth leather until he came to a small bulge. He pulled the key out. "I got it," he whispered.

"Hennricks, let me know if anyone is coming, "the Captain said. He held his hands out to Adams, who found the key hole on one cuff and turned the key. The cuff sprang open. Quickly, the Captain took the key out and leaned forward to unlock one of Adams's cuffs. "When you put it back on, keep the ratchets to the outside of the cuff, on the inside of your wrist. They'll look like they're on, but if you turn you wrist, your hand will come free." The Captain showed him how to do it and turned to loosen Hennricks's cuffs.

"Wait," Hennricks said. "Someone is coming!"

The Captain dropped the key in his back pocket and put his cuffs back on. He sat back on the chair as Q-Ball entered the office. "How's everything goin' out there?" the Captain said.

Q-Ball looked at him, frowning. Whatever Leon had told him to do, he wasn't too happy about it.

"People's gettin' jumpy. Leon wants to kill all you all. He says he knows you from way back. Says you shoulda let him burn."

"I was thinking the same thing," the Captain thought. To Q-Ball, he said, "I'll remember you for protecting us."

"Just doin' what I'm told," Q-Ball said. "Nothin' more. Things be turnin' to shit."

The Captain felt a knot rise in his throat. If negotiations weren't working and an assault was coming, a lot of people would be hurt.

"It won't be long now, 'fore somethin' happens," Q-Ball said, and turned toward the door. There was shouting outside. The door slammed open.

* * *

THE DAY WAS WINDING DOWN. Soon, the afternoon count would be taken, Gaines was handling that, and the second shift schedule would be posted.

Afternoons were usually pretty quiet. The mail had been delivered; those few inmates who got it regularly were the envy of the rest. Most inmates were taking a nap or sitting in their rooms or dayrooms, watching soap operas. The unit staff had completed their room shake-downs and pat-downs and were waiting to go home.

The Captain hadn't had time to check the School-Maintenance complex, and Lt. Gaines was busy with a drug investigation. He found Wilkins grabbing a soda out of the machine in the visit room.

"Just who I've been looking for!" the Captain said. "I'll take a diet soda. Don't be cheap! Buy a bottle!" He'd stolen that phrase from the two officers in the Control Center, who started their day at 6:00 a.m. and were locked in until their relief came at 2:00 p.m. Because of their isolation, they were known as mooches. The C.C. was self contained, surrounded by thick steel bars, the most secure area at North Woods. It was only possible to enter through a set of double doors controlled from the inside. As at Seg', the windows were "ten-hour glass; the solid steel walls extended far below the floor line. The officers of C.C. had access to fire extinguishers, air-packs, a separate air exchange unit, and two fully loaded twelve gauge shotguns. They monitored all the radios in the joint and communicated with other state prisons, as well as the County Police and the State Patrol. A bank of video monitors above them showed roadways, Segregation, and the barracks units. The C.C. looked like the command deck of the Starship "Enterprise."

The officers inside couldn't get to soda or snack machines, so they often solicited those passing by in the Administration Building to get things for them. No one escaped the notice of the "Evil Twins." Dick Becker had been the control sergeant longer than the Captain could remember, and at age sixty-three, he still had the bearing of the Army Airborne Ranger he'd once been. His cropped hair and droopy mustache reminded the Captain of the actor Sam Elliot. His easy manner hid the fact that he had spent long months in combat in various parts of the world. Becker enjoyed the solitude of the C.C., and so did his side kick, Jon Hilbard, a tall, lanky thirty-something who had spent years as a patrol officer. Each knew the other's job; sometimes even the other's unspoken thoughts. If you were on their good side, they left you alone. If you were on their bad side, you might receive a few unwanted radio and telephone calls.

Lt. Gaines was often their target, purely because they liked to mess with him. "Control to Oak 24," they'd say, knowing he'd gone to the staff bathroom with a newspaper, "what's your 20?" they'd ask, knowing he'd have to grab his radio and tell them where he was. Or they'd wait until he was sitting down for lunch: "Control to Oak 24, report to Admin. to ID an off-grounds trip." It would continue until Gaines would offer to buy them both a soda. Then, together, they'd chime: "Don't be cheap! Buy a bottle!"

With a sigh, Wilkins dropped the coins into the soda machine and pressed the button for diet soda. "I don't know how you drink this crap," he said, shaking his head and looking at the diet Coke with disgust. "This stuff will kill you."

"And I suppose the copious amounts of beer you drink is good for you?" was the Captain's retort.

Wilkins looked at the Captain and replied, matter-of-factly, "My Dr. says there's the same protein in a bottle of beer as there is in a pork chop. I don't like pork chops, but I do like me some beer!"

"To each his own." The Captain sighed, "We've got some time to kill. Let's go see what Hans and Guard Meister are up to. If we hang around here, heaven only knows what the talking heads will come up with!"

The Captain and Wilkins walked silently across the lot to the patrol van. Wilkins cranked the engine to a start, sighed, and took a drink of soda. "Man, a half-hour and we blow this dump!" He put the car in gear and headed toward the school. The Captain leaned against the headrest, eyes closed, planning his evening after work.

1:35pm

The school resembled hundreds of public schools across the nation. Its long halls were lined with lockers. The classrooms were decorated with ABCs, flash cards, magazine covers, and newspapers — like the classrooms at LeAnn and Marie's public school. The sounds rising from the classrooms, most days, were as pleasant as at any school: a grammar lecture, a video narration about WWII, the squeak of markers on a dry-erase board as a teacher demonstrated math equations. Each of the dozen rooms held fifteen students. Each student attended four classes a day, studying anything from basic literacy to college-level math. Most of the inmates were reading at about a fourth grade level, and their math skills were even lower.

Some inmates had never before had the chance to learn. Most came from broken inner-city homes where survival, not education, was the priority. Their schools had been havens for gang activity, and drugs, sex and booze had overshadowed their future.

In prison, the young inmates made the acquaintance of forty- and fifty-year-old 'bangers who were spending their lives locked up. If they didn't like what they saw, they took to school like fish to water. If they were too thick to notice their options, they dragged themselves to school, but not for learning. They were the problems, the ten-percenters. They went to school to make connections, to build a reputation, or to impress the parole board. Learning was the last thing on their minds.

In the school security office, Hans Van der Beeck and Floyd Meister were at their desks, talking about hunting and shooting. They were impressive marksman, members of the North Woods sniper team. Everyone called Floyd "Guard Meister" because he refused to let anyone tell him he was a correctional officer. "I'm a guard," he'd say with pride.

Guard Meister was a short, rotund red-head with a temper to match his height. He had joined the Marines at age nineteen, and had honed his skills as a sniper in Iraq during the first Gulf War. His found himself lying, one morning, at the edge of a primitive village. He had been waiting two days for a high-level target, an Iraqi officer who had "gone native." The officer stepped into view, Meister's observer confirmed his identity, and, as the officer stooped to relieve himself, Meister fired a single round. The officer collapsed and fell on the spot he had soiled. It was the first of many kills for Meister, some planned, most unplanned: young men, old men, even women and children. He had been forced to kill a boy of eight or nine years old, which a fanatic had wired with explosives and sent running toward a Marine post. Meister couldn't forget the terrified face of the child as he ran to a certain death and the look of pain and surprise when Meister's bullet struck him in the throat. That face and memory haunted Meister's dreams. Yet he had never stopped practicing shooting. Even now, he could shoot three rounds into a one-inch target in less than five seconds at four hundred yards — and that was after sprinting one hundred yards. At North Woods, he used a rifle much the same as what he'd had in Iraq — and what he still used as a recalled Marine reservist.

Meister's partner, Hans, had wavy black hair and a slight paunch. He was about fifteen years younger than Meister, and a foot taller, and he was equally skilled. He had taken first place in the handgun competition at the yearly State Police games.

"Hey, Cap, Hans says he's gonna get a trophy buck this year. Remember last year when he shot that little nub buck? It was so small it looked like a German Shepherd with two-inch antlers!"

"It was small, but it was tender," Hans said.

The Captain shook his head. "Did I ever tell you the joke about the three guys who died and went to heaven? St. Peter met them at the Pearly Gates and told them, 'We want you to be happy in heaven, so I need to know your interests.' He called the first guy over and said, 'I see your IQ is one fifty-five. I'll bet you like physics.' The guy said, 'you bet,' and St. Peter said, 'Well, welcome to heaven! You're not going to believe the lab we have here!' Then he turned to the second guy and said, 'I see your IQ is one thirty-five. You like computers?' The guy said, 'you bet,' and St. Peter said, 'Well, welcome to heaven! You're not going to believe our computers in Heaven!' Then he turned to the third guy, frowned a little, and said, "I see your IQ is forty-eight. Get your buck this year!?"

Wilkins, a non-hunter, guffawed. Hans cracked a smile. Guard Meister looked steadily at the Captain, unsmiling.

"What's the matter, Guard?" Wilkins asked. "Don'cha get it?"

"Oh, I get it!" Meister sniffed. "I can't help it if some people don't have the killer instinct."

"That's OK, Guard," the Captain said, "some of us don't need to kill something to reassure ourselves of our masculinity."

"Cap, be careful: You're using those multi-syllable words again and you know how that confuses Guard!" Hans laughed.

Guard Meister shook his head and cursed under his breath.

"When you gonna take us out and run our asses off again, Cap?" Hans asked. "We never had to run when Capt. Mills had the team!" Captain Mills had retired three years before. He was, only about five- feet-seven inches tall and weighed in at three hundred pounds.

"If you haven't noticed, Capt. Mills isn't here anymore. And when he was here, he wouldn't run anywhere unless there was cake at the end. Before I took over, you guys were like an old gentlemen's shooting club. It took you five minutes to line up a shot and take it! At least now you can shoot under stress, and make the shot in a couple of seconds."

It had been hard for the Captain to break the snipers' habit of slow deliberation. He'd pushed them to practice instantaneous decisions and shots, and while he knew they had the ability, he sometimes wondered whether, when it really came down to it, they'd make the right call and take the shot.

"Yeah, " Guard Meister said, nodding at Hans, "and Mills always brought food to grill!"

"That's because Mills wanted to make sure he had enough to eat. You guys are out there to shoot, not eat!"

"Well, it was a lot easier with Mills, when we didn't have to run before each shot and we had a good lunch. I'm too old for that running B.S.!"

"It's good for you," the Captain said. "I'm older than you, and I run right along- side of you. I'll bet if Sgt. Golden was out there, you'd run for her!"

"That's different!" he said. "Cupcake is worth running for!" For reasons the Captain could never decipher, Guard Meister adored Sgt. Golden, his "Little Cupcake."

"I don't know why you call her "Cupcake," Wilkins said. "Pound cake is more like it!"

"You just don't know a good woman when you see one!" Guard shot back.

"You just ain't right," Wilkins concluded.

"I'm going to try to schedule some training next month," the Captain said. "I've got teams from two different county sheriff's departments that want to train with us. They learned a lot from you guys last time."

The Captain was proud of his snipers. In the three years he'd commanded them, they'd taken first place every year in both the Corrections sniper competition and the handgun competition. The eight men on the team ranged in age from thirty-one to sixty and had an average of fifteen years seniority. They worked posts ranging from patrols to maintenance sergeant. Of the eight, three were military veterans and all were dedicated hunters. The Captain would trust his life to any one of them.

"I don't know why we have to train cops," Guard Meister huffed. "Any of 'em would still give me a ticket if they had a chance!"

"Hell, Guard, "the Captain said, "I'd give you a ticket if I had a chance, you old Crank!"

"That's why I don't drive where you work. I wouldn't want to give you the satisfaction!" Guard Meister huffed.

The bell signaling class change rang, and the Captain heard classroom doors opening. Guard Meister and Hans rose to go. All of the officers and teachers helped monitor inmate movement. The Captain and Wilkins stood outside the office door, watching the surge of convicts. They looked like any group of students. It was easy to forget that each had committed a crime: theft, rape, murder and everything in between.

They walked in groups, chatting. There was safety in numbers, and if anything happened, it usually happened in front of a staff member. The Captain had learned long ago that inmates needed to save face; in almost all fights, one of the men didn't want to fight. To save face without losing teeth, it made sense to start a fight within sight of a staff member. That way, the fight would be broken up quickly.

Another bell sounded and the inmates disappeared into classrooms. A couple of inmates jogged up the hallway, late. "C'mere." Guard Meister gestured one over to him. "You're tardy."

"Man, I just got done at the dentist. Call up front and check."

"What's your excuse?" Guard Meiser asked, holding up a hand to stop the other.

"Who, me? Why? I just overslept a little late."

"Overslept! It's almost two in the afternoon! How could you oversleep? Get your butt in the office, the both of you. I'll call Health services for you, " he said to the first inmate. "But you," he pointed at the second, "you're definitely gettin' a write-up."

"It's gettin' to be that time." Wilkins looked at his watch.

"What time is that?" The Captain grinned. "Miller time?"

"There you go again! You tryin' to tell me something?"

"Nothing you don't already know," the Captain said, as they headed out.

CHAPTER XV

"Get his ass out here," Leon yelled. "We want them to see what we gonna do!"

Q-Ball pulled the Captain roughly to his feet and threw him face first against a wall. An inmate he couldn't see grabbed his other arm, and together, they dragged him out the door and through the barracks, with a row of taunting inmates on each side. He was hardly able to keep his feet under him. But while their attention was not on his hands, he worked to free them from the restraints.

"Motherfucker, we're walkin' you to da doe," the inmate at his right arm said, in the unmistakable thick voice of Leon. "We be done talkin' cause no ones be listenin'! It be time to show 'em we be done fuckin' around! If'n you does anythin' stupid, I'll cut yo' froat! Y'un-nerstan'?"

The Captain nodded, "yes." Something cold and sharp touched his Adam's apple.

Leon leaned in close to his ear and whispered, "I been lookin' forward to shankin' yer ass! It's jes about time for a little payback!"

As he was led through the unit, the Captain saw that the inmates had destroyed the officer's stations: inmate files were strewn everywhere. Several inmates were bruised and bleeding, victims of fellow convicts who had taken out their vengeance on those they considered

194

weak or snitches. From the back of the inmate bathroom, someone screamed, pleaded, "I'm not a snitch! Please stop! It hurts too much!" The Captain didn't want to think about what was being done in there, and with the shank to his throat, he had other problems. He saw no sign of Sgt. Golden and shuddered to think of what she might be suffering.

He could feel Leon's breath, hot on his neck, stinking of stale cigarette smoke. He turned, caught a glimpse of ragged scar tissue, skin pulled as taunt as a drum. Leon's lips had been seared off in the fire, and his teeth, yellowed from tobacco, had nowhere to hide. His mouth formed a permanent "O," as of surprise or fear.

"That's right, Motherfucker," Leon whispered. "This is what you did! If'n you hadn't fucked with me and thrown me in the hole in the first place, none of this would have happened. I wouldn't look like a freak, and you wouldn't be dead today."

"Leon, it doesn't have to end this way," the Captain said. "If you try to kill me, you'll be dead. They'll shoot you." The Captain hoped that Guard Meister was on the rifle covering him. Guard Meister wouldn't hesitate.

Leon laughed in his ear. "I ain't gonna die today, Motherfucker, you are! I gots these other stooges here doing my shit!" He pointed to Q-Ball. "As soon as I cut you, I drop behind yo' big ass like a stone. Aint no one gonna shoot a man already on the ground. That ain't legal! You gonna die, I gonna live. I may look like a freak the rest of my life, but I'll be a happy freak knowin' I iced yo' ass." The Captain felt the cuff loosening on his wrist.

Leon pushed him toward the door to the yard. He could feel the inmate trembling. The Captain realized that he was trembling too. Fear was their bond. Or maybe, the Captain thought, he's trembling out of anticipation. Anticipation of the kill.

The door opened into the early evening light, and the Captain stood in the doorway, held firmly between Leon and Q-Ball. In the distance, he could see the road where he'd watched the deer earlier in the day. It seemed as though it was years ago that he had watched them vanish into the freedom of the woods. He brought his focus back, to the SWAT team fifty yards away, their weapons pointed at him and the inmates. The building was ringed by armed men, and somewhere, unseen, were four two-man sniper teams, their scoped Remington 700 rifles trained on the head of the man behind him. If Leon made a move to kill him, one of the four men on the rifles would shoot. Within micro-seconds, a 168 grain .308 caliber boat-tailed hollow point would slam into Leon. Q-Ball too. The shots would destroy the inmates' brain stems. Their heads would burst like a gallon milk-bottle dropped to the floor. Blood, brains and bits of skull would explode out the back of their heads, covering everyone within a ten-foot radius. The Captain took no solace in the thought.

"I will survive!" he told himself. "I will survive!" He could feel one hand coming free of the cuffs. Leon shoved him forward, still holding firmly to his arm.

"I done told you Motherfuckers to back off!" Leon screamed. "I'm gonna kill the Captain if'n I don't see ya backin off! I aint bullshitting!"

The SWAT Team stood its ground, not giving an inch. "Unit Sixteen inmates!" Capt. Halfbeck called through the bullhorn. "You are committing an illegal action! All inmates who wish to come out are to exit the side door with your hands over your head. You will not be harmed! If you stay in the building, you're actions will be illegal and you will be prosecuted! Any inmate not involved in this situation can leave the unit now!"

Leon's arm tightened around the Captain's throat. The Captain could feel the inmate's heart hammering, the inmate's stale breath blowing harshly on his cheek. "You gonna die, Motherfucker," Leon whispered. "I'm gonna cut your throat and feel you die."

Out of the corner of his eye, the Captain could see a group of inmates running from the building, their hands over their heads. "Get on the ground! Get on the ground!" Halfbeck called. Ingalls, the old con from the Captain's yard crew at Meadows, threw the Captain a glance; there were tears in his eyes. Another old con, Chrystalman, lay on the ground with the surrendering inmates; the Captain had planned to stop in and see a picture of his grandkids. As the SWAT team members sat Chrystalman up for cuffing, he looked sadly at the Captain shook his head, and mouthed "goodbye."

*   *   *

2:00pm

"WHAT YOU GOT GOIN' AFTER work?" Wilkins asked the Captain, as he steered the van away from the school building.

"The way I look at it, about an hour from now, I'll be beating the hell out of my Lazy Boy! Marie doesn't get home from school until about four; I have to take her to piano lessons at four-thirty. Maura is gone until about five, so I'll have a little quiet time. LeAnn has to work tonight. The rest of us will probably just grab a burger somewhere and go to the volleyball game. Exciting, huh?"

"LeAnn still work at the restaurant?"

"She's a hostess. She says it's not too bad, now that she can wear regular clothes. She doesn't like the white uniforms."

"I worked in a restaurant when I was in high school," Wilkins said. "I hated it. After that, I worked selling shoes for a while, then got a job at the out-board motor plant. I was making good money." Wilkins glanced at him thoughtfully. "You had a pretty good upbringing didn't you?"

The Captain laughed. "Good and bad. My dad was liked to hunt and fish, and when he wasn't doing that, he drank. He had a good job as a toolmaker and made decent money, but Mom still had to work outside of the house, and money was tight. When I was a kid, we did all kinds of stuff together. When I turned fourteen, my Mom got cancer and I pretty much ceased to exist as far as my Dad was concerned. He was so wrapped-up with her, that I was more of a nuisance to him than anything else. I'd always been a hellion, so that didn't help much. We lived out in the sticks, and there wasn't much to do. When I was about eight, my older brother and I got new BB guns. We hopped on our bikes and rode around shooting out yard lights at farmhouses. Of course, we got caught. Dad made us each cut a switch off of the willow tree in the backyard, and I was already crying as I cut the switch. 'Do you know why I'm doing this?' he asked, slapping the switch on his leg. I told him I did. 'Are you ever going to do it again?' he asked. I told him no. 'All right, then,' he said, setting the switch behind the garage door, 'I guess we'll keep this just in case there is a next time. Go to your room.' We had to pay for the lights, of course."

"Did you ever do it again?" Wilkins asked.

"Nope, but I did get the switch a time or two for other stuff! Grandpa was more easy-going than Dad. He owned a dairy herd, and with the crops he produced, he was able to keep his business going through the Depression and into the 1960s. He had his own truck, and in the summers he'd let me ride along on milk runs. We were going down an old dirt road once, when I was seven or eight, and he let me sit on his lap and steer. The cab was open to the back, and he had a bunch of watermelons there, along with the milk and eggs and juice. I saw a big pot hole in the road and deliberately steered toward it. We hit it before Grandpa could grab the wheel, and one of the watermelons bounced up and hit the ceiling. It just exploded! There were red bits of watermelon streaming down the inside of the truck, and seeds and green rind everywhere! It was all over us, too. At first, Grandpa was mad, but then he burst out laughing. "That one was for Archie Dagmoore," he said. "He's a Democrat, so I guess he'll just have to pay for his melons like I'm paying for his mistakes in Washington!"

Wilkins smiled and ran a hand through his hair. "Terri has an appointment at the doctor at 4:00, and I'm going along. The doctor says we should be able to hear the heart beat by now."

"You'll never forget it," the Captain said. "Maura and I hadn't planned on children, but nature eventually took over. When I heard LeAnn's heartbeat for the first time, I couldn't believe it. She was alive in there! Maura had thirty-six hours of labor with LeAnn, and the first thing she said to her was, "Oh, Sweat-heart, you're just what we wanted!" I cried more than LeAnn. Just wait until you hear that heartbeat, Dave. That's when it'll become real to you. That's when you'll know why you're here."

"It'll be nice to know why I'm here," Wilkins said. "I just sometimes wonder why I'm **here**?" He looked out the window.

"I guess I wonder that sometimes, too," the Captain said. "For some people, it's just a job. I guess I do it because I want to make a difference."

"Do you think any of us really can make a difference?"

"Sure. If I didn't think that, my whole career, a big chunk of my life, would be wasted."

"I don't know. Sometimes it seems that we're nothin' but babysitters for a bunch of losers."

"Yeah, but haven't you ever met an inmate who you know has the potential to get out and do something good?"

"I guess so."

"Come on, Dave. You can think of someone who's gotten out and made it."

"It's a lot easier to think of the ones who didn't."

"Yeah, but that's only because you keep seeing them again and again. Think about all the guys you never see again. They're out there somewhere, raising a family, making a living."

"Either that or they're dead."

The Captain laughed. "True, but the reality is that a lot of guys eventually get it and stay out. I know you've made a difference in someone's life. What about JT?"

JT was a cocaine addict who had become an armed robber to support his habit. He was in the drug treatment program when Wilkins was working the program unit, and he worked in the kitchen. At the age of thirty-seven, he was also one of the older students working toward a high school diploma; he had trouble with math. "Man, C.O., this stuff be gettin' me down!" he told Wilkins one afternoon, waving a math worksheet. "I be just about ready to quit."

"What's the problem?" Wilkins bent over JT's desk.

"It's these here 'quations. How'm I suppose ta know anything abouts interest that's compounded semi-annually at seven and three-quarters percent, and what my monthly payment would be after I puts fifteen thousand dollars down-payment on a two hundred thousand dollar house with a thirty-year fixed loan? I ain't never had more'n five or six hundred dollars at any one time in my whole life! And they's talkin' 'bout two hundred thousand!"

"Let me look at it." Wilkins took the math book and sat down with JT. They looked at the "'quations" and worked their way through the problem. "OK," Wilkins said, "now figure it out if your down payment was only ten thousand dollars."

As JT worked, Wilkins watched and did his own equations. A couple of times, he could see JT was getting stuck, but he sat back and let him work his way through it. Finally, JT brought his paper to Wilkins. "The way I figure it," he said, "is that I'd be payin' mor'n I'd make if I was a doctor!" He showed his work to Wilkins; their answers were the same. From then on, anytime JT had a school problem, he went to Wilkins and they figured it out together. Within, six months, JT had earned his H.S.E.D.

When JT tranferred to minimum, it was the Captain who ID'd him out. In chains, JT grabbed the Captain's hand and held onto it before stepping onto the bus. "Cap'," he said, "on the night my Momma died, you came down to the unit and told me. It meant a lot for me to hear it from you, instead of just gettin' it on the phone. I want you to know I 'ppreciate that you took your time to tell me." With his coat sleeve, he brushed away a tear. "You tell Wilkins that I 'ppreciate everything he done for me. I'll miss you guys, and that crank Murph too."

"Take care, JT." The Captain put his hand on JT's shoulder. "And don't be coming back. There's a whole lot of living out there, and you've missed enough of it."

* * *

"I guess I helped JT," Wilkins said, "but that was a few years ago. I haven't seen or heard of him since he transferred out."

"That's the point," the Captain said. "If you haven't heard of him, maybe it's because something you said or did helped him stay out. Maybe, because of you, he's doing OK."

"Maybe he's doing OK " Wilkins said, nodding. "Either that, or he's dead."

CHAPTER XVI

6:36 p.m.

"*Target in sight,*" *Guard Meister said, peering through the sights of his scope. He was lying on the roof of the school building two hundred yards away from Unit sixteen, and had his crosshairs centered on a spot just below Leon's upper lip. A tangle of emotions welled up in him, and he tried to press them down: the face of the Iraqi boy at the moment he was hit kept swimming to the surface of his consciousness, messing with his concentration. He had killed because it needed to be done, Meister told himself, just at it would probably need to be done today. If Leon was going to kill the Captain, Leon needed to die. There was no wind, and Meister had his scope at the right setting. If the barrel of his Remington 700 sniper rifle wavered even a quarter of an inch at this range, he'd miss Leon. He might even kill the Captain . . . . . but he wouldn't think about that. There was no wind, and he had his scope at the right setting. Leon was hurting his brother officer, and if he went any further, well, he was an eighth-inch trigger-pull away from death.*

Down in the yard, the knife pressed harder on the Captain's throat, and he felt fear rising in him — that he wouldn't see his daughters grow, that he wouldn't see them marry and have families, that he wouldn't hold Maura again, that he wouldn't be able to tell them all, one last time, how much he loved them.

"*All right, you Fuckers! Back off or we'll kill the Captain!*" *Leon yelled. " We got us a bunch of hostages, and we ain't afraid to kill one to show you we mean bidness!*"

A trickle of warm blood slid down the Captain's throat.

"No matter what happens, Motherfucker, I'm killin' you," Leon whispered. "Aint nothin' gonna save you." Leon pressed the shank into the Captains side, cutting into his ribs, and as the Captain flinched, he dropped the cuff from his wrist. Leon moved the knife back to the Captain's throat.

Across the yard, on the roof of the maintenance building, Walters, moved his scope a fraction from Q-Ball's face and watched Leon pressing the knife into the flesh of the Captain's throat. ""T-1, he's drawing blood," Walters radioed.

"Shit," Hans said.

Walters moved his scope back to Q-Ball, who held the Captain's arm in one hand, a shank in the other. The other two teams would wait until Guard Meister and Hans fired, then, within a millisecond, they'd send another bullet into the brain stems of Leon and Q-Ball.

"We see the blood," another team called.

Guard Meister said a short, silent prayer. "Please, Lord. Let me get the shot off before that mother-fucker kills my Captain."

"Team Leader to all shooters, do you have your targets in sight?" Capt. Schmidt radioed.

"Affirmative" came the response from each team.

Thorson radioed, "Command post to all teams, you have a "Green Light."

Capt. Schmidt verified the call as a "fail-safe" and relayed, "Sniper Teams one, two, three and four, you have a green light" — approval to kill. He thought back on his friend's prank that morning with the Baby Ruth, when neither had any inkling that the day would end any differently than any other. He felt sick to his stomach.

Guard Meister felt the air leave his body, as he waited to take his shot. He was seconds away from killing a man, and took no pleasure in it.

On the yard, the Captain had worked the handcuff off of his left wrist. He lowered his head as much as he could and tilted it off to the side to give the snipers a better shot. Then he dropped to his knees, grabbed Leon's wrist and struggled to break free." It's my only chance to live," he thought, "my only chance to go home."

He never heard the volley of shots.

* * *

2:03pm

"YOU OFF TOMORROW?" WILKINS ASKED.

"Yup. Today's my Friday. I'm off for the next four." The Captain worked split weeks, eight days on and two days off or seven days on and four days off. He hated it. "I don't have any plans for the weekend. I might go shooting one afternoon, then run and see my dad, but other than that, I plan on taking it easy."

"Must be nice, all that time off."

"I don't mind the time off, but it's a killer working seven or eight days in a row, and if I have training or I have to cover a shift for someone, it can be eighteen or nineteen days straight." It had been years before he'd even had enough seniority to take holidays off. He'd spent more Thanksgivings and Christmases in the company of convicts than with his family. His first winter working for the prison, when his mother was dying of cancer and he'd only been married for a few months, he'd ended up with double shifts both on Christmas Eve and Christmas day. Maura had gone home, just like in college, to spend the holidays with her family. So, there he was, twenty two-years-old, kissing his parents goodbye and driving through sub-zero weather to spend Christmas Eve surrounded by inmates.

The moon was high and sparkled off the snow, illuminating the countryside. He'd never felt so alone, as though there was nobody even aware that he was alive. He passed a farmhouse, its driveway full of cars, and through the front window, he could see a family gathering. He passed a small country church and saw families walking hand in hand to celebrate the birth of their Savior. And then, for the last several miles, nothing — except a dilapidated old farm house. It had always looked to him as though the farm was abandoned, but as he got closer, lights took shape. Off in the distance, in the middle of a small grove of trees by the rundown house, a Christmas tree shone brightly, topped with a bright, white star! There were no lights on in the house, only the tree shining alone in the dark woods.

He slowed his car, smiling, realizing that even though he was by himself, he wasn't really alone. He was loved by his family and by his God. Life was good.

"Never mind the damn schedule, Dave," he said. "I'm spending the next few days basking at home. Ain' nothin' better!"

"I hear you on that, Boss!"

2:04pm

"Wanna stop and see how the rookie is doing over in sixteen?" Wilkins asked.

Unit Sixteen, the barracks unit, held one hundred sixty inmates all of whom were new to North Woods, having transferred from other prisons. Many were Maximum Security inmates who had worn out their welcome elsewhere.

"I suppose we should look in on him," the Captain said.

"It's bustin' his cherry fast, putting him in Sixteen," Wilkins said. "Ever since we opened it, the other joints have been sending us their trash. Ya think the rookie'll look you in the eye?"

"Let me guess: You told him I had a glass eye."

It was a standard joke: "The Captain has a glass eye. He's real sensitive about it, and he gets mad if he thinks you're looking for it. Don't *ever* let him catch you looking or he'll go ballistic! Don't look him in the face at all, if you can help it."

Usually, the Captain caught on right away. The rookie would be talking *to* him, but not looking *at* him. Depending on how frazzled the rookie seemed, he'd let him off the hook right away or play along. He'd set a stern look, remove his glasses, and rub his left eye. Or he'd close his left eye, as though winking, and after a moment or two, lift the lid with his finger, muttering under his breath.

"It was either that or tell him to ask about your sister, the stripper. I didn't think he'd swallow that one."

"Probably not. Let's check out industries, before we hit Sixteen."

The Captain and Wilkins fell silent as they headed for the inmate textile shop. Only twenty-five minutes left in the shift; it was almost time to go home. "Code One! Unit 16!" the radio squawked. "Code One! Unit 16! All responding units reply!"

Wilkins swung the van around and stepped on the gas, as the Captain radioed a response.

"Fuckin' Rookie probably set off his alarm by mistake," Wilkins said, looking at his watch.

"Maybe," the Captain said, "at least I hope so."

CHAPTER XVII

6:37 p.m.

THE SHOOTERS HIT THEIR MARKS. Guard Meister and Hans each saw his target explode in a red mist, as Capt. Halfbeck moved in with his SWAT teams. Several inmates outside the building dropped to the ground, suddenly eager not to show the slightest resistance. Unarmed riot control units moved in, handcuffing and searching them before shoving them roughly into waiting vans; within two hours, most would be in segregation in other prisons.

At the same time, the SWAT teams hit the building. Bergman and Murphy crashed through a side door with a crayon-shaped battering ram, and tossed in flash-bang grenades. Capt. Halfbeck fired a volley of tear gas, and the team entered, Murphy at the lead. "GET DOWN! GET ON THE FUCKING GROUND!" they screamed through their gas masks. Inmate Dunbar appeared from around the corner holding an improvised club; his eyes met Murph's at the moment Murph fired the shotgun, tearing a hole in Dunbar's chest. Dunbar's body dropped to the ground like a stone.

In the corner of the room, beyond the dead inmate, lay the naked, bloody body of Sgt. Andrea Golden. Murph flashed on Sgt. Golden's son, a police officer in Milwaukee, but he put him from his mind. He couldn't stop for Sgt. Golden; his job was to find the hostages. Murph jacked another round into the chamber and, stepping over the body of the dead inmate, ran to the social worker's office, mashing in another shell, as he ran, to top off the magazine.

As they entered the office, a lone inmate stood to greet them and was met by a butt-stroke from Sgt. Bergman's Ruger Mini-14. He went down in a mass of blood and tissue, his nose and jaw shattered.

Armed officers poured into the dorm, fanning out in pre-planned directions, shouting orders at terrified inmates, slapping cuffs on, and starting pat-downs.

Adams and Hennricks had done as the Captain told them; they were on the floor, Adams behind a computer desk, Hennricks in a corner opposite the door.

Bergman, spotting Hennricks, saw a frightened young man — the same age as his daughter — who needed to know he was safe. He let his weapon drop on its sling and pulled off his gas mask. "It's all right, son, " he said, "I ain't gonna let no one else hurt you." He held out a gloved hand, pulled Hennricks up, and they embraced like father and son, tears streaming down their cheeks.

Adams stood up behind the desk, shaken and bruised, and looked at Halfbeck. "How's the Captain?"

A quarter-of-a-mile away, in the administration building, Lisa heard the volley of shots as clearly as if they were outside her window. She dropped a mug of coffee and sank to her knees, tears flowing. No one had been able to reach the Captain's family.

LeAnne had gone straight from school to her job as a hostess and was busy seating customers and flirting with a new host, a big seventeen-year-old who, like it or not, reminded her a bit of her dad. She had to work until nine, and after that, she hoped to con her dad into watching a rerun of "The 70s Show." It was a weekly ritual for them, a chance to connect.

Marie had skipped school and was at her best friends' house watching a "Twilight" movie marathon. She knew her parents would have a fit; her Dad would ground her if he found out. But she couldn't help it; she enjoyed the risk. If she was home by four so, no one would be the wiser. Her dad would take her to the dreaded piano lessons with Ms. Hoffstetter, a stern, thin woman with long delicate fingers that seemed to stretch from one side of the keyboard to the other. After the lesson, Mom would meet them for a burger and the volleyball game. Marie hated school, piano lessons, and everything she had to do with her parents. But she loved them, and she was more like her dad than she cared to admit.

Maura had gone to her studio in the country, her "world away from the world." She had turned her cell phone off and put a "House" DVD in for background noise and was painting from a photograph she'd taken last year at Yellowstone National Park: a bear in the middle of a flowing stream. The bear was lying on his back, embracing the cool water as it washed over him. She added some indigo blue to the water, and after a few brush strokes, stood back to look at her work. It was almost complete, and she pondered what was missing, knowing that it would eventually come to her. She had a couple of hours to work, knowing her own "bear" wouldn't be home for a while and that he would most likely enjoy the quiet of his home for an hour or so. She realized suddenly what the painting needed; a few droplets of water on the bear's muzzle, to show his delight in the world, in the moment. She worked on the droplets, eager to make the world right. For that moment, the world *was* right.

CHAPTER XVIII

ON THE COLD, CONCRETE ENTRANCE outside of the unit, the bodies hadn't been moved. They lay where they had fallen, awaiting examination. Pictures would be taken, measurements made and the entire scene documented on video. It was clear that Leon and Q-Ball were dead, their heads shattered by the high powered bullets. The contents of their hollowed-out skulls splattered the walls behind them; their caved-in faces were indistinguishable. Leon's body lay slumped over the Captain, who was covered with bits of blood and brain. His shirt, neatly pressed and white only hours before, was saturated with blood. The jagged cut on the Captain's throat looked as though it had been chain-sawed, stretching almost from ear to ear.

Sgt. Golden's body was taken out first, covered by a folded flag that had been hastily taken from the flagpole in front of the prison. As the body passed between the two lines the officers had formed, each held their hands in a salute. The sounds of muffled crying were heard, but each officer held their salute until the body was loaded into the coroners van.

Under the pile of bodies, the Captain stirred. Lt. Gaines was the first to notice. Over here!" he screamed to the ambulance crew, as he began digging through the mangled mess to get to his Captain. The Captain's eyes were closed, tears welling in the corners like puddles on a country road. His left hand still held Leon's wrist, the wedding band his wife had placed on his finger more than twenty years ago shining under the grime. Blood from his throat spread out and ran down the front of his shirt, over his gold name tag. The gurgle of blood escaping amplified his breathing. He opened his eyes slowly and became aware of Lt. Gaines. Gaines had stripped off his white shirt and was pressing it tightly to the Captain's throat with one hand, while he held the Captain's hand with the other.

"Don't worry, Brian," he said to the Captain, "you'll make it through this. The sheriff has all of his deputies out getting your wife and kids, and they'll meet you at the hospital. It's over now." As they loaded him onto the stretcher, Gaines reassured him, " I'm going to ride there with you."

As he faded from consciousness, the Captain was filled with peace. His thoughts were filled with Maura, LeAnn, and Marie. He recalled the love of his parents and Grandparents and his mind was overwhelmed by the blessings life had given him. He was lifted into the waiting ambulance. It's lights and sirens screamed into the cold autumn night and echoed through the woods as the crew worked feverishly to save the life of a man they didn't know, the life of a man that was loved, hated, feared, and respected. The life of a man no different from the life of any other person on earth, except to those who knew him and loved him. Behind him, the walkway would soon be washed clean of the blood of Leon, Q-ball and the Captain. Three men that wanted nothing more than to be home.

THE END